"A beautifully written and illustrated fantasy adventure packing emotional punch."

—**Jon Robinson**, Author of *Sunshine and the Full Moon*

"Absolutely brilliant! From the compelling storyline to the beautiful illustrations, this book draws you in from the very first page. This story is full of delightful characters, including grieving Olivia, helpful Diego, and a forest full of adorable talking animals. Each page pulls you deeper into a spellbinding plot about a young girl who discovers not just a magical forest but powerful lessons about nature, life, death, family, and friends. This charming yet provocative tale feels ancient and fresh at the same time: a contemporary fairytale as unforgettable as any of the classics. The story is mesmerizing, making this powerful and poignant tale destined to become a modern-day favorite."

—**R. Scott Boyer**, Author of the Bobby Ether series

"Enchanting! This beautifully written and illustrated tale transports readers to a magical land where they will root for young Olivia to 'be the hero' in a quest to save herself, her friends, and her troubled world. Inspiring for readers of all ages."

—**Susan Diamond Riley**, Award-Winning Author of *The Sea Island's Secret* and *The Sea Turtle's Curse*

"Danielle Koehler presents a poignantly written, beautifully illustrated tale that will enchant children seeking to better understand themselves and make sense of the complex world they share with others. The story is captivating, and it packs a powerful message that children need to hear. Young people coming of age will learn how to discover, then harness, their inner strength and turn it into a force for good. They will come to better understand the adults who love them. *The Other Forest* should be at the bedside of all pre-teens, who will read it and then fall asleep dreaming of how they can join forces with others to become a hero."

—**Sandra Stosz**, Vice Admiral, US Coast Guard (ret.), and Author of *Breaking Ice & Breaking Glass: Leading in Uncharted Waters*

"Danielle Koehler brilliantly brings to life wildlife conservation in her new book *The Other Forest*, in which a teenage girl discovers a strange forest while searching for her beloved lost pet. Drawing you in from the first page, Koehler takes you on a beautiful journey through a magical, animal-filled world, full of emotional turmoil and important life lessons on caring for the natural world and its animal inhabitants. A powerful story of love and loss, heartbreak and healing, that will be enjoyed by young readers and their parents alike."

—**Madelon van de Kerk**, Professor of Wildlife Ecology at Western Colorado University

"*The Other Forest* by Danielle Koehler is a beautifully written fantasy for all ages. Her vivid storytelling and gorgeous illustrations not only provide the reader with entertainment, but also send a clear message; the earth, its ecosystems, and wild animals are vulnerable to the actions of the human race. Through the eyes of the characters, the reader is able to perceive this threat and will hopefully be inspired to take action. Loved this book!"

—**Julie Hartz**, Volunteer at Sonoma County Wildlife Rescue and Audubon Canyon Ranch's Living with Lions Program

"Danielle Koehler's debut novel is stunning. *The Other Forest* introduces Danielle Koehler as a writer and illustrator to be reckoned with. Koehler's engaging story and her beautiful artwork plunge the reader into the enchanting world of the Patagonian rainforest but also into the enchanted world of 'the other forest' where animals speak and spirits live. Exploring the depths of fear, anxiety, and even terror, Olivia, the protagonist, finds a secret place where she is challenged and comforted, embraced, and restored to face the life awaiting after her father's death."

—**Eleanor McCallie Cooper,** Author of *Dragonfly Dreams*

"Haunting and mystical, this book will transport readers to faraway places. The charming illustrations add to the magic."

—**Linda Oatman High,** Author of *As Far as Birds Can Fly*

"Danielle Koehler dazzles us with a novel that gravitates between fantasy, self-discovery, and the management of emotions in a world that has endangered childhood and natural ecosystems. *The Other Forest* is a beautiful book that puts the spotlight where it should be and brings to life unforgettable characters aimed to change your life for the best."

—**Wendolín Perla,** Founder of Perla Ediciones

"A wonderfully engaging and brilliantly illustrated book filled with fantasy, adventure, and excitement. The messages about conservation, mindfulness, friendship, hope, and faith are inspiring. *The Other Forest* is a joy to read!"

—**Pam Siegel MPH, MFT, and Leslie Zinberg,** Authors of *Grandparenting: Renew, Relive, Rejoice*

"*The Other Forest* is a unique and refreshing young-adult story that encompasses different cultures, a love of nature and animals, and beautiful author-created graphics. It's filled with touching anecdotes that can help young readers embrace how to move on from and even find sacred meaning in the death of a parent. Koehler writes in such a way that her protagonist will inspire you regardless of what age you are. *The Other Forest* has life and conservation lessons that we should all learn from again and again so we can rekindle the Energy and better love the Rudas and Newens around us."

> **—Sydney Scrogham**, Author of the Guardians of Agalrae series

"*The Other Forest* is a beautifully illustrated and engaging magical journey that takes the reader along a wonderful, action-packed nature adventure in a fantasy forest hidden within the real world while encouraging a love for wildlife conservation and the Spanish language—a nice, easy read."

> **—L. J. Litton**, Author of *The Arcanum, Bradley Gordon's First Adventure*; Former Executive Director, NATO NCIA; International Public Speaker, Writer, and Scuba-Diving Enthusiast

"A delightful romp through a fantasy wonderland . . . and beautifully illustrated. In the midst of a painful loss, Olivia learns to deal with the anguish and honor her father in the process. A book to be read by middle schoolers and parents alike with bountiful lessons to be learned."

> **—Robert A. Saul**, Professor of Pediatrics (Emeritus), Author of *Conscious Parenting: Using the Parental Awareness Threshold*

DISCLAIMER

This book is fantasy. While Newen and Ruda allow the children to touch them, I strongly urge you to **never approach, feed, touch, or attempt to ride a wild animal.**

Remember: the best way to protect wildlife is to respect their space and let them be free.

The Other Forest
by Danielle Koehler

© Copyright 2021 Danielle Koehler

ISBN 978-1-64663-462-0

Published by

 köehlerbooks™

3705 Shore Drive
Virginia Beach, VA 23455
800-435-4811
www.koehlerbooks.com

THE OTHER FOREST

DANIELLE KOEHLER

VIRGINIA BEACH
CAPE CHARLES

To Newen, Ruda, Tucu, and all the other injured,
displaced, and orphaned wildlife worldwide.

And to the people who dedicate their lives to protecting them.

1.
Welcome to the Ring of Fire

THERE WERE ONLY three things Olivia knew about Lenca:

1. Her grandparents lived there. (She hadn't seen them in years.)
2. The people spoke Spanish. (She didn't.)
3. It was at the literal end of the earth. (She had to turn a globe upside down to even find it.)

Olivia slumped against the car window, watching the deep blue of the Pacific Ocean blur past. At home, she could spend hours watching the waves crash, but unlike the sparkling turquoise of *her* ocean, this one looked dark, cold, and empty. There were no dolphins, or surfers, or kids boogie-boarding. Nothing but sad emptiness stretching into infinity.

Unsticking her curls from the misty glass, Olivia dropped her gaze to the book in her lap:

VOLCANOLOGY OF CHILE

It was a recent airport purchase that her mother had hoped would cheer her up. As much as Olivia hated to admit it, her mom was right—at least a little. According to the introduction, Chile had more than five hundred active volcanoes, mostly due to its location smack-dab on the Ring of Fire, sandwiched between the Peru-Chile Oceanic Trench in the west and the Andes Mountains in the east. A perfect recipe for volcanic activity.

"Did you read about *Volcán Calbuco* yet, Livy?" asked a cheerful voice from the front seat.

Olivia kept her eyes glued to the pages. She hated being called Livy. That was what Dad used to call her. He had a nickname for everyone: Livy or Liv-Bug for her, Captain Redbeard for himself, and Peppy Pepa for Ma, who was always smiling. Even now, after everything, she still wore that stupid grin.

"On a clear day, you'd be able to see the top of it over there." Ma tapped the window to their left, not noticing Olivia's silent treatment.

Olivia stared out at the thousands of prehistoric trees climbing up the mountain slopes before vanishing into a thick white mist. The forest looked like something ripped out of the pages of a dark fairytale about witches and ancient magic. She vaguely remembered some old legend her grandmother used to tell her about a strange goblin-like creature living in the forest. It made sense why people here might believe that, but Olivia was sure it was only a myth, something made up. She was having a hard enough time imagining a real-life volcano hiding back there, let alone mythical creatures.

Her curiosity getting the better of her, she flipped through the book until finding a photo of a bumpy, snow-covered volcano. *Calbuco,* read the text, *is an extremely explosive stratovolcano in the Lakes Region of southern Chile. Once considered to be among the most active volcanoes in the country, it has remained dormant since its last eruption in 1972.*

Olivia let a smile slip as she reread the line *extremely explosive stratovolcano.* Those were the best kind, like Mt. Vesuvius in Italy and Mt. St. Helens in Washington State. Ever since she'd studied them in Mr. Hughes' Earth Science class last year, she'd become a *tiny* bit obsessed. She had read everything she could find about the townspeople of Pompeii who never seemed concerned with the looming mountain peak, or all the earthquakes they were all too used to. Until one day when they awoke to a cloud of ash.

If there was one thing Olivia had learned, it was that no matter how long a volcano pretended to be a sleepy little mountain, sooner or later it was bound to wake up and remember what it really was.

Olivia snuck a peek at the rearview mirror, which reflected Ma's watchful eyes. Snapping back to a scowl, she reminded herself that no matter how undeniably cool the nearby volcanoes were, she must show absolutely zero interest in being here. If she stuck to this plan, Ma would soon see that this was all a huge mistake, and they'd move back to Virginia in no time.

Virginia. Home! Where she had friends, like Jill and Mandy and Eli and Lilli. And all the other Scouts. And her Shooting Sharks teammates. And—

A loud snore startled her. The culprit, her dog Max, was splayed out next to her, belly-up and fast asleep. Olivia scratched him in the secret spot that only she could find. Right on cue, his foot sprang into action like a lawnmower revving up. Olivia smiled. *At least I still have you,* she sighed.

"Look, they're about your age!" Ma pointed out the window at a group of boys playing soccer next to a small chapel with a weird pointy roof. "Let's say hi!"

Olivia shot her a horrified look. Right as she opened her mouth to speak, a *HONK-HONK* rang out of the car. One of the soccer players froze mid-kick and began jumping up and down, waving at them. Another player immediately stole the ball from him. The first boy's teammates threw their hands in the air, a few of them glaring at the offending vehicle.

Olivia slid down in her seat, hiding her burning cheeks from sight. *Ma just had to give me the worst first impression, didn't she?* Not that it mattered, since she was doomed to a friendless existence here anyways because of the whole "language-issue," which is what Miss Judy used to call it during their *totally* normal weekly counseling sessions.

But still. She preferred not to add an embarrassing-mother issue on top of that.

Five minutes later, the car parked next to a wooden cabin with a tall trail of smoke puffing out its chimney. In the yard, several black and white hens roamed between the ferns. Olivia frowned. There was no fence or anything keeping them in.

"Remember this?" Ma twisted around. Her bright brown eyes were wide with anticipation, the same brown eyes that had been passed down to Olivia, although she would have preferred receiving her dad's light blues. All she'd gotten from him was a sprinkling of freckles on her cheeks and a tiny dash of fire in her hair.

Olivia raised one defiant eyebrow in response.

"No? Well, maybe you were too young," Ma continued as sweetly as ever. "Come on. Let's go in."

Olivia sighed. *So, this is it. Our new—*

She shook her head and began to pack her things into her backpack as slowly as humanly possible: Max's doggy treats and water bowl; the volcanology book; half a chocolate bar stashed for later. Only one thing left, but he was a little too big to fit in her backpack. Olivia leaned in and booped Max on the nose. He blinked at her, yawned, and dropped his head back down. Clearly the sleeping pills they'd given him for the plane ride hadn't worn off.

"Come on, Max. If I have to go in, so do you." Olivia tugged on his legs, but he refused to budge.

Ma walked by carrying a big black suitcase and laughed. "Here in Chile, we call that '*por la razón o por la fuerza*.'"

Olivia dropped Max's limbs. "English, please, Josefina," she snarked.

Ma rolled her eyes in the same annoyingly playful way she always did when Olivia called her by her real first name. She banged on the front door and called back, "You know you're going to have to actually learn Spanish now, right?"

Before Olivia could respond, a short round woman flung open the door. She was covered in flour from the plaid apron tied around her waist to her head, where clumps of white dusted her short, black hair. Olivia's grandmother looked mostly as Olivia remembered her, with a few more wrinkles and rolls here and there.

"*Hola Pepa, mi hija preciosa!*" she squeaked, throwing her arms around Olivia's mother and kissing her on the cheek.

"*Hola, mamá!*" replied Ma.

The two women happily chit-chatted for a few moments until Olivia's grandmother turned to face her.

"*Hola, mi princesa!*"

Before Olivia could frown at being called a princess, she was scooped into her grandmother's plump arms and given one big kiss on the cheek. "*Hola, Abu,*" she groaned.

Having emerged from the car, Max stretched his paws out in front of him, shook the sleep from his body, and promptly trotted into the house.

Abu released Olivia, shrieking something about that "*perro*" being in her "*casa.*"

"*Mamá, te dije,*" said Ma.

"*Pero no me dijiste,*" Abu began to argue.

Olivia's head shot from one woman to the other, waiting for someone to explain. But they kept speaking Spanish until Olivia's mother placed one thin finger on Abu's lips, flashed her charming Peppy Pepa smile, and said, "*Max es de Olivia. Son inseparables.* Okay?"

Abu opened her mouth once more, but with a quick glance at Olivia, she gave one grumpy nod, and that was it.

Inseparables. That was easy enough to understand. And what a perfect word to describe Max and Olivia. Ever since the day she had found him abandoned in the state park and convinced her parents to keep him, which may have taken a *tiny* amount of begging and crying, they'd truly been inseparable. And boy was she glad that she'd found him when she did, as he was the only thing getting her through all this.

As soon as Olivia stepped inside, she inhaled the smell of baked bread and melted cheese. It was undoubtedly coming from the old wood-burning stove that sat in the middle of the room. That didn't seem like a normal place for a stove. But then again, nothing seemed normal here.

Unlike her bright and beachy home in Virginia, everything here was bathed in boring shades of beige and brown. Olivia scanned the cabin for the smallest pop of color, but everything from the roof to the floor was covered in wood or wool. Finally, her eyes landed on the couch, where a suspiciously bright neon-pink ball of yarn sat next to two cushions embroidered with the most beautiful blue and orange birds.

After removing her oversized bomber jacket and boots, Olivia sat on the couch to examine the birds. The light from the stove bounced off their colorful threads, making their wings sparkle ever so slightly. They didn't look like any birds she recognized, which was saying a lot considering she'd received the Birdwatching Badge just last year.

As Olivia caught herself wondering, no, *hoping* to see these birds in the wild, Max jumped up next to her. Apparently, he'd already completed his investigation of all the new smells the cabin had to offer and was now ready for his third nap of the day. Olivia smiled as he curled into a neat little ball. Always the big spoon, she lay behind him and squeezed her fingers into his warm belly. Nestling her face into his neck, she closed her eyes, breathing in his chamomile puppy shampoo, which would lull her to sleep. Maybe then she'd wake up and this all would have been only a bad dream.

The front door flew open, and a pair of heavy boots stomped inside.

"*Pepa!*" boomed a man's voice.

"*Hola, papá!*" replied Ma.

Olivia peeked open an eye and was startled by the sight of the old man at the door. She hardly recognized him as her grandfather. His hair was now completely white and hung down by his shoulders. It matched the silver beard hiding the bottom half of his face. He wore a black beret, an olive-green fisherman's vest, and large rubber boots covered in mud. When he saw Max, his eyes lit up like Christmas morning.

"*Un perrito!*" He clapped his hands on his thighs. Max immediately jumped off the couch, greeting the old man with one long wet kiss. Not quick enough to dodge Max's helicopter tail, Abu squealed like a frightened piglet as it thwacked her leg.

Olivia's grandfather chuckled as he wiped the slobber from his cheek. "*Qué buen perro!* He is yours?" He held out his hand to pull Olivia up from the couch.

"Hi, Tata. Yeah, he's—" before she could complete her sentence, she was pulled into a big bear hug. When her grandfather released her, he bent to meet her eye level.

"How is my favorite *nieta*? I hear you a little... *gruñona*, no?"

"Grumpy," Ma offered as a translation.

Before Olivia could retort, Tata continued. "*Escucha* . . . first thing tomorrow, we go, eh, *a pasear en el bosque?*"

"Go for a walk in the woods," said Ma.

"I got it, thanks," replied Olivia, although she certainly hadn't gotten it at all.

"Yes," continued Tata. "It help clear your head." He poked her and winked.

Ma raised her eyebrows. "Papá, are you sure it's safe?"

"Of course! Don't be worry."

"But Mamá mentioned something about some attacks from—"

"Don't listen her!" he interrupted, shooting Abu an angry glare. "She think forest is full of *demonios como el trauco*."

Olivia's eyes widened. She didn't know what the word *trauco* meant, but it sounded like maybe the forest really *was* full of witches and ancient magic! Tata held a hand to his face to shield it from Abu's view, and with the other hand he drew a small circle near his temple while mouthing the word "*loca.*"

Olivia clamped her hand over her mouth to suppress a giggle. Abu scoffed, and Tata blew her a kiss, which she swatted away.

"So, were there attacks or not?" Olivia asked, unable to resist.

"Well, yes. But not . . . *ay, es que . . .* " Tata frowned, searching for his next words. "That many, many years ago! Before you born. So don't be worry. Nothing scary in forest now, not even one animal. All gone! Today I try fish and *nada!*"

Olivia frowned so deep it hurt. She knew she should be relieved that the forest was safe, or whatever, but she couldn't help feeling upset that there were no animals anywhere. She glanced at the beautiful embroidered cushions and felt her heart sink.

"How is that even possible? Where did they all go?" she pouted.

Tata placed his hands on his knees and motioned for Olivia to move in closer. "Hide. All of them," he whispered. "You help me find them?"

Olivia grinned and nodded, forgetting her zero-interest rule. Catching herself, she glanced nervously at her mother, who had her back turned in that moment. *Phew! Close one.*

"Good. Tomorrow we go." Tata smiled, patting Olivia on the shoulder.

Abu sighed. *"Tu sabes que hay algo malo en ese bosque."*

Olivia only understood the word *malo*, but the message was clear.

"Let's eat. I'm starving!" Ma interjected before Tata could respond.

They continued speaking Spanish all throughout dinner. The only thing Olivia understood, unfortunately, was the name George.

It was said in that same hushed tone that people used when they said things like, "I'm so sorry for your loss," and "if there's anything we can do." Though they never said Olivia's name, several worried glances in her direction confirmed her suspicion that they were also talking about her.

Unable and unwilling to participate in the conversation, Olivia resigned herself to angrily poking at the slimy brown seaweed on her plate. It was cut into bite size pieces and sprinkled with onions and herbs, none of which managed to mask its terrible flavor. She swallowed as much as she could and tried to give the rest to Max, her faithful garbage disposal. But even he wouldn't eat the stuff.

The others were eating Abu's homemade *empanadas de pino.* Though they smelled delicious, Olivia had been forced to pass, as she recently made the decision to never eat a dead animal again. Abu appeared quite distressed with this news. After rummaging through the fridge, she found one leftover container with no meat. As she dumped the *ensalada de cochayuyo* on Olivia's plate, she mumbled something that sounded like *"morir de hambre . . . "*

As Olivia helped clear the table, she caught Tata sneaking scraps of food to Max. "Tomorrow you come with us. Yes, you SMELL animals. *Siiiii. Vamos al bosque!"*

"Basta!" yelled Abu. She had turned in time to see Max catch a piece of sausage. She pointed at Max and Tata, then outside, yelling something that Olivia assumed was a threat to kick them both out. Out of breath, Abu concluded her angry speech with, *"tú obsesión con ese bosque. Ojalá lo talen todo!"*

Whatever Abu had said, Tata did not like it one bit. His face flushed as he kicked out his chair and stomped out of the room. Olivia looked at Ma to see if she would offer a translation, but she just nervously smiled and scooped up as many dirty plates as she could hold.

At last excused to go to bed, Olivia slipped under the covers. She was so tired from all the travel that she didn't even mind the lumpy pillow or musty-smelling sheets. Drawing circles over Max's tummy, she wondered what Abu had said that made Tata so angry. But of the thousands of words she didn't understand, the ones that kept clawing their way back into her head were *demonios como el trauco*. What was a *trauco*? Too tired to rummage through her suitcase to find her dictionary, she rolled onto her side and turned off the light.

Whatever it meant, tomorrow she would find out.

2.

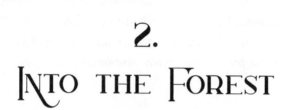

Into the Forest

THE NEXT DAY dawned with perfect conditions for a walk in the woods. The early morning sun spilled through the treetops, speckling the ground with spots of gold. Olivia smiled at the sky, breathing in the crisp spring air and rejoicing in all the wonderful sights and smells of nature. As she spied the curly gray moss spilling out of the trees like spaghetti, she realized something odd. Everything here looked strangely similar to a state park back home. Like that squirrel peeking out of a hollow in a pine tree, and that bright red cardinal landing on a branch. As odd as it was, she knew one thing for sure—Tata had been so wrong. This forest was full of animals!

As Olivia and Tata rounded a bend in the path, a large white house appeared before them. It also seemed familiar, with its front door and window shutters painted bright blue. A silver van was parked in the driveway with a license plate that read R3DBEARD. Olivia froze. This wasn't a similar-looking house. It was *her* house. She was home!

Squealing with glee, she sprinted toward it.

As her toes bounced off the first stones of the long cobblestone driveway, the ground began to tremble. Olivia turned to grab hold of Tata, but he was no longer there. He wasn't anywhere in sight. A sharp, hot panic flooded her. Her pulse quickened, rising to the rhythm of the earth shaking beneath her feet. From somewhere behind her house, the ground ripped open, and a large dome-shaped mountain peak rose, blocking the sun.

Olivia held her breath, her heart drumming in her ears. She knew that mountain peak. It was in every book on volcanoes she'd ever read. And she knew what would happen next.

In an instant, a massive ash plume exploded upward, turning the sky dark. Bolts of lightning twisted like glowing vines through the angry pillar of gray and black growing larger by the second. From the volcano's mouth, a fiery liquid spurted into the sky before dripping down its sides.

Then, the front door of the house opened. Out stepped a man with hair almost as bright as the lava. *Dad.* As quickly as Olivia's heart rate had risen, it stopped completely. It was as if everything had frozen, and there was nothing in the world but her and him, smiling and waving in slow motion, completely unaware of the dangerous scene behind him.

A loud CRACK snapped Olivia out of this daze. A huge chunk of the volcano's side had broken off, sending a landslide of rock, ash, and lava crashing downward. She knew she couldn't possibly outrun it, but she didn't care. Jolting into action, she sprinted as fast as she could.

It was close. Coming closer. Her dad held out his arms to her, welcoming her home. She pumped her legs, lungs bursting, but the driveway stretched on and on as the landslide of lava raced toward them. It was nearly at the house, a flowing stream of molten red. *No! I should have reached the house by now. I should have saved him by now. I should have—*

As she reached an arm out, a dark hooded figure stepped out from behind her father. It placed one long sharp claw around his neck and then—

"Olivia, breakfast!"

She jolted awake, her chest tight and fluttering as fast as a hummingbird.

A soft tap-tap-tapping on the roof told her it was raining outside. She looked out the window. This was not perfect walking-in-the-woods weather. And there was no spaghetti-slung moss hanging from the trees. No squirrels or cardinals or old silver vans anywhere in sight. This place was nothing like home.

It had only been a dream. Or a nightmare, more like it.

Her breathing calmed but the tightness in her chest remained.

"*¡A desayunar, princesa!*" squeaked Abu from below.

Olivia pulled off her sweat-soaked pajamas and threw them in an angry heap on the floor, as if they had been to blame for her nightmare. She put on a new pair of jeans and her favorite red and orange tie-dye sweater, which she had made in a Scouts meeting last year. But even as she descended the stairs into the living room, the heavy feeling of despair clung to her like a weighted blanket she couldn't shake off.

She sat and forced a smile before dropping her gaze to the table. In the middle was a small wicker basket holding a half-dozen pieces of bread. Olivia plucked one out and broke it open with her thumbs. A hot vapor cloud leaked out, scalding her. She threw the bread on her plate and sucked on her burnt thumb.

"Ah, yes. Be careful. Your Abu's bread is *caliente como lava*," said Tata. They were clearly still angry with each other, as Abu turned up her nose and he pointed his entire body in the opposite direction.

"After breakfast," Tata continued, still chewing a piece of bread, "we go out."

"In the rain?" Olivia asked.

Tata glanced out the window and waved it off. "This nothing. Gone in hour or less. Here it rain, then stop, then rain, then stop." He snapped his fingers every time he said the word *stop*. "Funny weather here. You see."

And he was right. By the time they had finished breakfast and Abu had gotten out the big bag of flour to start making other baked goods for lunch, the rain had disappeared.

"You see? Now go put shoes and we go."

Abu beat a mound of dough with her fists and mumbled, *"viejo porfiado."*

"Vamos!" Tata boomed. And with that, he was out the door with Max fast at his heels.

As Olivia ran to put on her precious bomber jacket and boots, Abu yelled, *"Espera!"* and scampered down the hall. She returned holding something the exact same violently bright shade of pink as the ball of yarn on the couch. Olivia swallowed her horror as Abu unraveled a long, knitted scarf with a fluffy round pom-pom tied on each end.

Abu thrust it around Olivia's neck and pulled it tight, practically strangling her. *"Ay, qué linda mi princesa!"* She squeezed Olivia's cheek, dusting it white with flour.

Olivia mumbled, *"Gracias!"* and turned toward the door. But once again, she was stopped from leaving. Ma placed one small hand on Olivia's shoulder and stared down at her with her large brown eyes like a concerned mama bear.

"Hey, I know this is a big change, and it's been hard on you. But I'm so happy you're giving it a chance. Tata is really excited, and I think you're going to love the forest." She tried to tuck one of Olivia's knotty curls behind her ear, but Olivia pulled away. Ma sighed.

As Olivia turned to open the door, she heard Ma whisper behind her, "It'll get better, I promise."

Olivia whipped the door open and ran out without looking back. She was furious. How dare her mother say that! As if it would all magically be okay again after one lousy walk in the woods? What's worse, it sounded like she didn't even believe it herself. She was only doing her annoying Peppy Pepa routine, trying to make everyone else happy. But Olivia wasn't going to take it anymore. After she got back, she would have to sit with her and explain that none of this was okay. Olivia wasn't going to pretend like it was, or ever would be again.

Olivia continued fuming until she reached Tata at the end of the driveway. He was puffing out smoke rings from a short wooden pipe as he waited for Max to fetch a stick. When he turned and got a glimpse of Olivia, he nearly choked on his tobacco. Olivia raised an eyebrow, confused, but then she remembered the fluorescent monstrosity hanging around her neck. Tata's laughter was so contagious that Olivia soon felt herself relaxing until a grin erased her long frown.

Olivia pretended to pet the fluffy scarf and joked, "Do you like Pinky? She's my new pet snake."

"*Precioso!* But why she on fire?"

Olivia giggled and began to yank off the scarf.

"Leave it," said Tata. "Keep you *calientita*. Your Abu want make you something. I tell her, 'Make it green. Olivia like green.' But she say '*Verde es para hombres!*'"

Olivia rolled her eyes. "Green is NOT just for men! She keeps calling me princess. I am NOT a princess."

"Ah, no? What are you then?"

Olivia hesitated before responding softly, "I'm the hero."

"Hmm?"

Olivia knew he had heard her, but she repeated, "I'm the HERO!" with more confidence. Dad had always told her, "Be the hero!" like a little motivational chant. She hadn't said it aloud for a long time, but something about Tata reminded her of Dad a little bit. Enough so that saying it now felt good, somehow.

Tata nodded. "Yes, you are!"

The farther they walked down the dirt road toward the deep green forest, the fewer houses appeared along the way. The clouds floated by in clumps, with enough pockets of clear sky to catch a glimpse of the magnificent snow-covered mountains in the distance. Olivia was equally relieved and disappointed to not see anything resembling a volcano.

Before the road ended, one last house appeared on the right. A young boy was looking out the window, waving at them. He cracked it open and yelled, "*Hola, don Pancho! Van al bosque?*" Without waiting for an answer, he added, "*Puedo ir yo también?*"

"*Sí, obvio,*" said Tata, followed by another something-or-other that went completely over Olivia's head.

The young boy turned and ran from the window excitedly.

"He is Diego. He like walk with me sometimes. He is good boy."

The boy, Diego, flew out the door to join them. He was a little shorter than Olivia, his skin a little darker, his nose a little rounder, and his teeth a little more crooked. But all of this was eclipsed by his enormous smile. He wore a blue-knit sweater, which looked handmade, and beat-up sneakers that were probably hand-me-downs.

"*Es tu nieta?*" he asked excitedly.

"*Sí*, granddaughter. Her name is Olivia. We speak English with her."

The boy's dark eyes lit up. "My . . . name . . . is . . . Diego," he said, pausing between each word. "I . . . have . . . eleven . . . half . . .years!" He flashed Olivia a big grin, proud of himself.

Olivia suppressed a giggle. "Hi. I'm Olivia, and I'm twelve."

"I . . . saw . . . you . . . car... I . . . play . . . *fútbol.*"

"Oh, right!" Olivia blushed as she recalled her mother honking at him. "Yes, I saw you. I play soccer too, actually."

"Oh, yes? Good! *Quizás—*" Before Diego could finish his sentence, Max appeared from around the bend and jumped directly onto the boy's chest, knocking him over and covering him in licks.

"Max, no!" yelled Olivia as she tugged at his collar.

Diego giggled as he stood. "It okay! I always want dog, but *mi mamá dice que no* and *en vez de eso* . . . she give brother a—" he wiggled his arm like a worm before shuddering and sticking his tongue out in disgust. "Bleh! What, *eh, raza* . . . dog?"

Olivia bit her lip. The absolute last thing she needed was for Tata to report back to her mother that she had made a new friend here. But as much as she was determined to remain grumpy, she had to admit it felt good to speak to somebody her own age. Plus, he was asking about Max, and Max was her favorite topic of conversation. Before she could stop herself, she cracked open her lips, and the words came spilling out of her like a slinky tumbling down the stairs.

"You mean what breed is he? We don't know. I found him as a stray. We call him a *boxasaurus* because we think he's got some boxer in there. Mixed with who knows what else to give him those stripes! Weird looking, right?"

Diego raised his eyebrows in confusion, and Tata burst out in laughter.

"Slow down," said Tata. "Need be more patient."

"Oh, right." Olivia deflated, instantly embarrassed by her outburst of excitement. "He's a mutt."

Diego stared at her blankly.

"Mutt? No? Hmm . . . " Olivia thought for a second how to translate the word mutt. She shrugged and gave it her best guess. *"Mixto?"*

"Ah, yes!" Diego nodded and yelled, "Like me!" He pointed to himself with his two thumbs and grinned.

"We are all mutts here," replied Tata.

"What do you mean?" asked Olivia.

"Oh, that our eh . . . *cómo se dice la sangre* . . . " Tata paused to think. "Our blood . . . is mix of Native peoples and European peoples from long, long ago. Many cultures, many time."

Olivia had never considered her lineage before. She'd definitely never thought of its history or culture or whatever. She just thought of herself as half Ma and half Dad.

Reaching the end of the road, they found a small dirt path that continued in its place. They ventured forward into the forest, leaving the sunshine behind the trees which surrounded them. On the ground were tiny plants painted white with frost, not quite tall enough to reach the sun's warm rays of light. Huge green ferns towered high above them, in between the skinny moss-covered trees that littered the forest. The cool spring air smelled fresh yet somehow had a distinct spiciness to it that Olivia couldn't quite place.

Gaping upward, Olivia was enjoying all the new sights and smells when she realized that one of her senses seemed to be missing altogether. It was suspiciously quiet. Not a single bird chirped, nor insect buzzed. The only noise was the soft rustling of a thousand leaves as the lazy wind blew through them. It almost sounded like the trees were whispering secrets, perhaps warning each other of trespassers.

Goosebumps formed on Olivia's neck as the word *trauco* crept back into her head. She had forgotten to ask about it, but the tree's whispers reminded her of its meaning. *Trauco* was the goblin-like creature haunting the forest; that's what Abu used to tell her. Could it be that Abu really, truly believed that the forest was full of goblins and demons? Tata had laughed at the ridiculous idea, but Olivia had to admit that something about this place gave her the creeps. With her senses now at high alert, she became acutely aware of the crunch of the tiniest twig, and even the sound of the damp soil compressing under her feet.

As they walked along, a trickle of water grew louder until eventually it was replaced by the roar of a rushing river. Olivia tried to peek through the trees on her right, searching for the source of the water, but the forest was too dark and dense to reveal anything.

As she continued reveling in these new sensations, her ears picked up another faint sound in the distance. This one was more familiar, although it felt out of place here in the forest. It was the high-pitched humming of a chainsaw.

As the noise grew stronger, Tata tightened his brow. He stopped and held out his hand for them to follow suit. *"Esos hijos de—"* He caught himself and looked at the children. "Wait here. I be back soon. DO NOT MOVE. *Entendido?"* He looked at each of them and watched as they both nodded.

And with that, Tata stomped off.

Now alone with no grown-ups to protect them, the forest became a little bit darker. Olivia tried to ignore the goosebumps traveling up her arms, reminding herself that she was not a baby who believed in ridiculous legends anymore. Tata had said there was nothing dangerous in this forest, not even animals. She was sure he was right.

And if he wasn't, she always had Max. She scratched him behind his ear and thought, *You'll protect us from whatever might be in here, right?*

As if reading her mind, Max commenced his famous *there's something here I must conquer* routine. First, he frantically sniffed the ground at his feet. Next, he shot up in alert position, the fur on his neck pointing up like a porcupine. And finally—

"Max, NO," Olivia commanded, lunging for his collar.

But he was already out of reach, sprinting into the distance.

Olivia's heart leapt to her throat. "MAX!" She screamed, already knowing it was too late.

There was no ignoring her fear now. They were only two kids, alone in a potentially demon-infested forest, with no grownups *or dog* to protect them.

Great. Just great!

3.
PULL, BREATHE, SHOOT

OLIVIA SHIFTED HER eyes toward her only remaining companion. Diego shuffled his weight back and forth. Was he as scared as she was, or was he just not used to standing still for long? Either way, she should probably start a conversation with him, but she had no idea how much he would even understand.

Seeming to notice her hesitation, Diego pointed to the right and asked, "How you say?"

Olivia squinted toward the direction he pointed. There wasn't much to choose from. "Uh . . . trees?"

"*Treeees*," he repeated, rolling the *r*. He stomped on the ground. "How you say?"

Olivia frowned. "Dirt?"

"*Dert*! And this?" He pointed back to the right and waved his hand. "How you say?"

Seeing no end in sight, Olivia shot back, "River, but hey, let's play something else, okay?"

Diego's grin stretched to his ears. "Play! Yes!"

Olivia looked around. What could they play that required no talking or running around? Not much. Great! They'd be back to the *How You Say* game in no time. Olivia sighed and put her hands in her pocket, where her fingers hit something soft and round in the bottom corner. She pulled out whatever it was.

"What is that?" asked Diego, eyes wide.

Olivia smiled, recognizing the brown leather pouch. She slipped her fingers inside and scooped out a handful of colorful glass orbs.

"They're marbles."

She didn't remember putting them in her pocket. They were always kept in the special box in the hall closet, along with the big green World War II bomber jacket she was wearing. Both items had belonged to her grandfather, who had passed them on to her father, who, knowing how much she loved them, must have put the marbles in the pocket.

Olivia snapped out of it, realizing this wasn't the time or place to think about that. She peeked at Diego. He wasn't looking at the marbles at all. Instead, he was staring directly at her, as if trying to read the mix of emotions on her face.

Olivia quickly cleared her throat, trying to compose herself as if nothing had happened. "Oh, uh, right. I guess we can play with these, as long as we're careful."

She scattered the marbles on the ground and used her finger to draw a circle in the dirt around them. Almost done, she now had to find . . . there it was! Her favorite shooter marble, the one with teal and orange stripes swirling together like an ocean sunset. Carefully placing it on the ground outside of the circle, she lined it up and flicked, hard. *Clack!* One of the other marbles shot outside the circle. Olivia smiled, picked it up, and set it aside in her victory pile.

"Now you try," she said, handing him the shooter marble.

Diego flashed a devilish grin as he pulled out a slingshot from his pocket. In two seconds flat, he had loaded the marble in the leather sling, and, before Olivia could stop him, shot it into the circle. It hit the ground with a loud *CRACK* and shattered in two.

"NO, you IDIOT!" Olivia yelled, her anger exploding out of her faster than she could control. She plucked the two broken halves from the ground. A teal swirl on one side and the orange swirl on the other. Cradling them in both hands, a wave of cold sadness washed over her, putting out the raging flame that had burned inside her.

"Look what you . . . you don't even . . . how could you?"

"*Perdón,*" Diego whispered.

Olivia inspected the glass shards in her palm. Maybe she could glue them back together, but it would never roll the same. It was as good as trash. Nothing left to do, she collected the remaining family heirlooms from the ground and gently placed them back into the leather pouch for safe keeping. She then took a deep breath and turned toward Diego, who stared at the ground with the same sad puppy eyes that Max always had after he was caught doing something bad, like digging in their neighbor Miss Jane's garden. It worked every time Max did it, and as much as Olivia hated to admit it, it was working now. Diego looked so miserable and pathetic that even she felt bad for him.

"Hey," she said. "I'm sorry I yelled at you. It's okay. Let's forget about it."

Diego continued fidgeting with his slingshot, refusing to look at her.

Olivia sighed, already regretting how nice she was being to this annoying marble murderer. "Can I see your slingshot?" she asked, holding her hand out.

Diego's face shot up, his dark eyes glowing and crooked teeth on full display as he passed her the toy. He pointed to his chest and stated proudly, "Me . . . make!"

"You made this?" Olivia inspected the impressive Y-shaped piece of wood and thick rubber band in her hands. "This is really cool. Will you teach me to shoot it?"

Passing it back to Diego, Olivia watched as he placed a small stone in the sling and closed the cloth around it, pressing together with his thumb and forefinger. He then pulled it back, hard and tight, and released. Faster than her eyes could follow, the stone zapped against a tree and bounced to the ground.

"You see? Easy!" He passed the slingshot back to her.

Olivia tried to imitate him but soon discovered that it was much harder than it looked. Every pebble she chose refused to cooperate, flinging itself lifeless to the ground at her feet. She was getting frustrated when Diego tapped her shoulder.

"Estira, respira, dispara." Diego mimed pulling back the sling, breathed in a long breath and held it for a moment, then mimed letting go. He exhaled. *"Así."*

Olivia nodded and gave it another try. It was far from perfect, but the pebble landed a little farther this time. After several more tries and lots of half-English words of encouragement from Diego, Olivia got the hang of it. She pulled the rubber band back with all her strength, her elbow shaking slightly from the pressure, took a deep breath, held it in, and let go.

Thwack!

It hit the mark.

"YES! Take that!" Olivia yelled as she high-fived Diego triumphantly. Several more successful hits and high-fives later, Olivia didn't even remember why she had been mad at him in the first place. In fact, she was having such a blast that she hadn't realized how much time had passed until . . . Max!

He still wasn't back. She was used to him taking off on his little adventures, but usually he returned in a few minutes, tongue out with that adorable dog grin, extremely pleased with whatever he had discovered. But there was no sign of him.

"That's strange," Olivia mumbled. "Maybe he got distracted by an animal."

"No animal here," said Diego.

"Well, he definitely smelled *something*." Another shiver ran down her neck, which she tried to shake off.

Diego's eyes grew large. He stood as still as never before, staring at the forest in the distance. For the first time, Olivia could tell that he was just as scared of whatever may be out there as she was. If only she had known him longer, then she could ask him to go with her to look for Max. But that wasn't the case, and the look on his face told her that this was something she needed to do on her own. Besides, she was sure Max was somewhere close by.

"Don't worry," said Olivia, feigning confidence. "Stay here. I'll be back soon."

Before the boy could protest, or she could talk herself out of what she was about to do, Olivia sprinted away.

"Max!" she yelled, scanning the dense vegetation on either side of the hiking trail. She was sure he hadn't gone far. He never did. Yet there was no indication that a dog, or any animal for that matter, was nearby. No leaves rustling or heavy paws pounding through the dirt. No angry birds warning him to stay away from their nests. Nothing. At least nothing that she could hear over the sound of the chainsaw.

Its humming grew louder until Olivia reached its origin. She darted behind a large tree, peeking out at a group of four men. Three of them were busy cutting down trees, while the fourth, her grandfather, was yelling and waving his arms around in the air like a madman. Paying no attention to the angry old man, the others continued piling up perfect little logs in the back of a large pick-up truck. Olivia felt a twinge of sadness. She had seen a similar pile of perfect little logs in her grandparents' cabin, sitting in a basket right next to their wood-burning stove. So that was it for these ancient trees. After who knows how many years, they would all soon turn to ash.

Judging by his red, scrunched face and wild hand gestures, Olivia guessed that Tata wouldn't be losing steam any time soon. It should be safe to continue a little farther. She studied the group of men a moment longer. When all of them had their backs to her, she bolted out from behind the tree and sprinted the short distance of the clearing until the trees closed in once more.

With the guard clear, Olivia slowed. The path soon became less obvious as nature began to eat its way inward, reclaiming the land that man had once cleared. She carried on, hopping over the many thick roots shooting out of the ground and ducking under all the sharp, low hanging branches.

Every so often she would pass by a gap in the trees on her right and catch a glimpse of the river whose constant symphony followed her along. Its water was a brilliant shade of turquoise blue that she had never seen before. It rushed downward at an impressive speed, crashing into protruding boulders and spitting out bits of sparkling white foam. It was breathtaking, but unfortunately there was no time to stop and admire it. She had to keep moving.

An idea popped into Olivia's head. She cupped her hands around her lips, filled her lungs with as much air as she could, and let out a long howl. "HOOOOOO-WOO!"

It had been a long time since anyone had used their special family call. Too long. It had started as Dad's way to call Max when he routinely wandered off, but its effectiveness soon turned it into an all-in-one family homing beacon, used to easily locate each other in the mall, theme parks, or any other crowded space.

The loud call echoed throughout the forest, bouncing off trees and rocks, but still there was no response. At least nothing besides the trees' constant whispering, which seemed to grow louder by the minute. Olivia trudged onward, but she was already getting tired. Her muscles were starting to strain, and she could feel little beads of sweat begin to form on her forehead. But the worst feeling of all, and the one that was becoming harder to ignore, was the bone-chilling tingle that ran up the back of her neck every time she remembered that there might be something out there watching her.

4.
THOUSAND-YEAR-OLD TREE

"MAX . . . WHERE ARE you?" Olivia repeated, barely audible. *Maybe he's gone back. Maybe I should too.*

As Olivia weighed this decision, she pushed past one more large fern, and there it was, the most colossal, magnificent tree she had ever seen. From its size, she guessed it must be hundreds of years old, maybe even one thousand. It was so wide that even if every girl in her Scouts troop held hands to form a human-chain, they still could not have wrapped their arms around it completely.

Olivia stood with her mouth open. The tree didn't look like a pine or oak or anything else from back home. Its bark was the same burnt orange color as the muddy clay from Gramma L's backyard creek. And like that clay, this tree also appeared to be sculpted, as if someone had very carefully carved out individual slabs of wood here and there. Olivia's hungry eyes devoured every inch of this cracked and knotted wood upward for more than fifty feet without seeing a single branch protruding from its sides. High above the canopy of trees, thousands of leaves exploded outward like a giant green mushroom cloud reaching for the sun.

As Olivia continued to gaze upward, the whispering returned. Stronger than ever, there was no more pretending that it was the rustling of leaves. There were words being spoken, a nonsensical spattering of words, but words nonetheless. There were distinct notes like *leee* and *vaaa* and *yaaa*, and it sounded like they were being whispered into her ear. She twisted about, searching for the voice, but there was no one.

Another noise pierced her ears. At the base of the tree, the massive spider web of roots creaked and groaned as they uprooted from the ground, untwisting themselves right before her eyes. They slithered around like tentacles, rearranging themselves until grinding to a halt in the shape of a twisted archway. Behind this, a small tunnel appeared, burrowing into the ground.

Olivia took a small step forward. She had an unexplainable yet irresistible urge to investigate this mysterious tunnel. She took another step, then another, and before she knew it, her feet were out of her control, as if some invisible force were pulling her forward. As soon as she reached the archway, she stopped and exhaled, feeling a huge wave of relief.

Slowly, she bent and peered inside the opening. It was too black to see anything. She leaned in another inch and called out.

"Hello?"

Helloo.

Hellooo.

Helloooo.

The word bounced around in the dark before fading out.

As Olivia considered turning around, a bark echoed out from deep within the abyss.

"Max!" Olivia yelled. Stretching out her fingers to guide her way, she crawled blindly into the dark. Once fully engulfed in black, the familiar creaking and groaning of the roots started again. Before she could turn to look, the ground dipped down, propelling her forward. Olivia slid headfirst through the mud as if on one of the rides at the waterpark. It was dark and bumpy and scary, and before she could finish her thought, the slide ended.

She fell.

Wind in her hair, clawing at the dark, howls fading out behind her, she fell.

Still, she fell. Farther, farther down.

She fell for so long that the familiar rollercoaster stomach sinking feeling disappeared, replaced by a sense of weightlessness. Realizing that she'd been screaming the entire time, Olivia swallowed one giant gulp of air. Not a second later, she struck freezing cold water. The force of the impact was so strong that it nearly knocked all of the air out of her. Clamping her mouth shut, she looked toward the surface, toward salvation. A single ray of light shined from high above, illuminating the bubbles escaping her mouth. She stretched out her arms, desperate to reach that light. Kicking her feet as hard as she could, she willed her body to move upward, yet a current continued to pull her down.

As Olivia sank, the light from above became dimmer. Her body began bending backward in a circle like it had when caught under crashing waves at the beach.

She remembered a day like this, when she'd been dragged around in the whitewater, the violent ocean waves throwing her body into so many underwater somersaults that she no longer knew which way was up. She'd been trained to relax and wait for the wave to calm as

there was no use wasting strength attempting to fight it. The current would always pull her to the surface after a few seconds.

But staying calm in this dark, cold place was easier said than done. Her natural response was panic.

The wings of a thousand butterflies beat against the inside of her belly as Olivia struggled to hold what was left of her breath. Just as she was about to lose hope and release the butterflies, her body came to a stop. Now completely upside down, she saw a second light shining toward her. Almost out of air, Olivia felt her body being pulled toward this new light source. Closer and closer it came. Just as she couldn't hold her breath any longer, she emerged, gasping for air.

Drinking in the longest, deepest breath of her life, she filled every corner of her lungs with as much air as she could get. Unclenching her stomach, the last of her butterflies fluttered away. Slightly more relaxed but still extremely disoriented, Olivia looked around. *Where am I?*

It appeared to be some sort of underground cavern. She dog-paddled to the wall in front of her and touched it. It felt rough and splintery like tree bark. *Am I still inside the hollow of the tree?* Laying back in the water, she floated with her arms and legs splayed, letting the light from above splash on her face. It was too high, much too far to climb. There had to be another way out. But there was nothing but dark walls. She twisted herself backwards and saw a shore, so close, inviting her to reach it.

Olivia swam toward the land, not knowing where it would lead, but not seeing another option. When her fingertips struck the soft mud of the shore, she pushed down with all her strength and crawled out of the water. Steadying herself, she squinted into the tunnel ahead of her. It was pitch black.

"Max?" Olivia whispered. His name echoed throughout the tunnel.

"*Ashh Essss Oeerr Eaarr,*" replied phantom whispers.

Olivia shivered, but not from the freezing cold. Extending her right hand to the side, Olivia cautiously searched for the edge of the tunnel. Very slowly, she traced her fingers along the bumpy roots that stuck out from the muddy wall. After a while, her eyes adjusted to the darkness. The farther she walked, the brighter it seemed to become. But there didn't appear to be a source of light, and she still couldn't see the far end of the tunnel. It was almost as if the roots themselves were glowing. But that didn't make sense.

Two yellow orbs of light blinked on in the distance. Olivia paused to observe them, but as quickly as they had appeared, they went out. She took another step forward. Again, they appeared before her, closer now, until once more they disappeared.

"*Ashhh Wehhh Arthh,*" the whispers hissed.

"Who's there?" yelled Olivia, bracing herself.

This time, it wasn't a nonsensical whisper that responded, but a real, full voice.

"Whoooo's there?" replied the voice.

Olivia wrapped her arms around herself a little tighter. "My . . . my name is Olivia. Can you tell me your name?"

"Tucu," replied the voice, ever so deliberately.

"Tucu? That's an . . . interesting name." Olivia continued to take tiny steps forward. "Do you speak English, Tucu? Can you understand me?"

"Of course I can understand you," replied Tucu in a deep tone that Olivia assumed was male. "Just as well as you can understand me."

Olivia sighed in relief. As strange as this all was, it was so nice to find someone—or something—that spoke English. Maybe Tucu could help her.

"Mr. Tucu, I'm looking for my dog. Have you seen one come through here?"

"I have seen most things, strange things, things that shouldn't be here," said Tucu. "I can see that you are quite frightened by the darkness. There's no need for that here, when it's the darkness inside you that is the real danger."

"Darkness . . . inside me?" Olivia asked.

"*Arrrk Nesss,*" echoed the whispers.

The hairs on the back of Olivia's neck shot up. She took a step back, distancing herself from whoever or *whatever* this strange voice belonged to.

"Oh, no, you don't want to go backwards!" said Tucu. "You need to move forward."

"*Ashhh Wehhh Arthh,*" the mysterious whispers repeated in high notes much different than Tucu's baritone voice. Olivia continued backing up little by little until the yellow orbs disappeared again. She took a gulp of courage and spoke once more.

"Look. I don't mean to bother you. I'll be gone soon," Olivia said as she continued to scan the tunnel for any sign of a presence. "Please, tell me if you've seen a dog run through here."

"Well, yes," said Tucu. This time his voice came from behind her.

Olivia twisted backward and there they were, the two glowing orbs, or eyes, as she now realized, staring back at her. They were sideways now, one on top of the other, as if he were clinging to the side of the tunnel like a monkey or, perhaps, a goblin! Olivia shuddered as the word *trauco* flashed into her mind once again. It couldn't be. It was a myth! *Just a myth. Just a myth,* she repeated to herself, inching backwards.

"As I said, you need to move forward!"

Swoosh! A burst of wind hit Olivia's face.

"Go on! Forward!"

"*ASHH WEHH ARTHH!*"

A second burst blew into Olivia, almost knocking her over. She covered herself with her arms. Several more came at her in rapid succession, pushing her forward one step at a time. By the time the twenty-something burst of wind hit her, Olivia couldn't take it anymore. She put her hands out in front of her and ran, blind, as fast as she could. She kept running until the ground slowly inched upward and the inside of her eyelids began to change colors from black to brown to orange.

Olivia stopped, out of breath. Peeping one eye open, she was flooded all at once by brilliant shades of greens and golds. She was back in the forest. It would have been a relief had it not been for the whispers. But they were still there, and much louder than before, like a constant humming from every direction. Olivia covered her ears to block them out.

"Ignore them," said the deep voice from the tunnel. "They always act up every time a newcomer arrives."

Olivia darted her head in every direction, searching for the voice. But there was no one there besides a large owl perched on a branch above her. His many feathers were brown and black and white, creating an intricate tiger-stripe pattern on his chest. On his head were two fluffy black horns jutting above his large, bright yellow eyes.

"Oh! A great horned owl," exclaimed Olivia. Forgetting all about the whispers and every other strange thing that had happened, all she could think in that moment was, *if only I had my camera to take a photo for Jill!*

And then, the strangest thing of all happened. The owl opened his beak and spoke.

"As much as I enjoy being called *great*, I am actually a *Magellanic* horned owl."

Olivia jumped backward.

"You're Tucu?" she said, now realizing that his large yellow eyes were the same ones that had followed her in the tunnel. "But . . . you're an owl! You're not supposed to speak!"

Olivia scratched the back of her head. Maybe she fell harder than she thought.

"Is that so?" said Tucu as he cocked his head sideways. "And who are you to decide who can and can't speak? What are you anyway? If I weren't mistaken, I'd say you were . . . but that can't be. It's impossible!"

Tucu spread his wings and leaped down, skillfully grabbing hold of a smaller branch with his large black talons. The branch bobbed, but the owl's head remained perfectly stabilized, as if disconnected from the rest of his body.

"Are you—" The owl squinted his large eyes as if he were studying every single freckle on her face. "Are you a human?"

"What do you mean? Of course I'm human," Olivia replied.

Tucu's narrowed eyes expanded to the size of golf balls. His striped chest feathers puffed out, and his wings and tail fanned out into a circle behind him.

"Oh no, this is not good! Not good at all!" said Tucu frantically. "I must inform the others. They're not going to believe—"

"Wait!" Olivia yelled, watching the owl prepare to take flight. "Can you please tell me where you saw my dog?"

"This *dog* animal is important to you?" Tucu twisted his head sideways.

"Yes! He's lost, and I really need to find him. Please!" Olivia took in a deep breath. As her heart rate calmed, she realized she was shivering. She hunched her shoulders inward and wrapped her arms around herself, trying to retain warmth.

Tucu swiveled his head, studying her once more. Then, without another word, he leapt off the branch and gracefully glided away. If Olivia hadn't seen it with her own eyes, she never would have known he left. His large striped wings made no sound. *So that was how he was able to move around so silently in the tunnel.* Olivia should have guessed it, since only owls were gifted with the trait of silent flight.

Before Olivia could take a step forward, the owl returned holding a long twisty green vine with a pink bell-shaped flower at the end.

"Catch!" he said, dropping the plant to her. "Eat this."

"What is it?" Olivia frowned, inspecting the flower. The inside of its pink petals were speckled white. It was beautiful, but she had been taught not to eat anything from the forest unless she knew exactly what it was.

"It's a copihue flower. It will lift your spirits and heal your aches."

Olivia frowned. "If I eat it, will you tell me where you saw my dog?" Though still not totally convinced, she was pretty sure eating one flower wouldn't kill her.

The owl bobbed his head in agreement.

Olivia shrugged and plucked the flower off its stem. "Bottom's up!"

It didn't taste like much except a little rainwater mixed with a bit of honey. As soon as she swallowed, a slight warmth swelled in her stomach. It spread outward to her chest, arms, legs, and finally her head. The pain in her back and legs from her fall vanished. Olivia stared at the green vine still in her hand and then up at the owl in amazement.

"You see?" he said. "You'll need something much more powerful than that to heal the pain in your heart, though."

Olivia couldn't help rolling her eyes. "Oh, right, the darkness inside me and all that. So . . . my dog?"

"Ah, yes. I already told you where to find him. You must go forward." Tucu twisted his head completely backward. "He went north, toward the volcano."

"The volcano?" Olivia thought of the photo from her volcanology book. "Calbuco?"

"Yes, of course, but you should try to catch him before he gets too far. Not everything in this forest will be as welcoming as I am, especially considering what you are." The owl puffed out his chest feathers once more.

A look of alarm came over Olivia. "You mean those things that keep whispering at me?"

The owl hooted out a laugh. "No, not them! They're harmless! Can't even move. Oh, I shouldn't say much, but I'll tell you this. If you see a swarm of dark things flying about, run! I must go now, but perhaps we should meet again in time."

"Wait!" Olivia called. "Can't you come with me? What if I get lost?"

"Oh, I'm afraid I cannot. I have some important news I must deliver. But don't worry. Sometimes the only way to find yourself is by getting lost at first." With those last words, Tucu extended his checkered wings and took flight.

Olivia sighed, alone again in this strange forest. She looked in the direction that Tucu had indicated. *North. Here goes.*

5.
THE WAY FORWARD

THE FARTHER OLIVIA advanced, the denser the vegetation became. The trees grew tall and thin, reaching for whatever scarce rays of sunlight they could find. Thorny bushes shot out in every direction, threatening to rip Olivia's precious jacket to shreds. She carefully dodged under and around them, getting by with only a handful of scratches in her large puffy sleeves.

All the while, the unrelenting whispers followed her.

"*Shaaa Maaah Asssh.*"

"*Hooo Raaath Aaarth.*"

Olivia reminded herself that Tucu had said they were harmless, whatever they were. But their constant babbling made it hard for her to think straight. She snapped.

"Whatever you are, please, please be QUIET!" she yelled at the sky.

The whispers faded until not a single *ash* or *sha* was heard.

"Thank you," Olivia nodded, still not knowing who she was talking to, but grateful all the same.

Now, without the whispers bouncing around everywhere, Olivia noticed an odd sound. It was a delightful choir of high-pitched whistles and trills and buzzing and pecking on wood. The forest brimmed with activity all around her.

As much as she wanted to stay and listen to every animal present, Olivia knew she had to keep moving. Enough time had passed that Tata would definitely know she was gone. She had to find Max and return before he started to worry. Overhead, the pale blue sky was barely visible behind a multitude of branches. She had no indication which direction she was going. No visible markers, no volcano, no Northern Star, nothing. If she wasn't careful, she could easily end up going in circles.

Olivia stopped and pressed her palm against the damp green moss on a tree to her right. *Moss grows on the north side of trees, right?* She would have to follow it, as simple as that. She traced her fingers around the tree. But the moss grew on every side, from the roots all the way to the very last branch. *This isn't a normal forest.* No. She shouldn't have been surprised, considering not a single thing here had been normal. For whatever reason, this particular moss wouldn't lead her anywhere.

Olivia leaned against the sponge-like texture, letting the moss's soaked-up rainwater drip down her temple. This little bit of cold made no difference to her, as she was once again freezing from head to toe. It seemed the effects of the copihue flower didn't last very long. Not only was she cold, but she was tired, hungry, and thirsty and so, so alone. What she wouldn't give to have someone, anyone, with her right now. Surprisingly, the first person to pop into her head was Ma. To have her rub her back or comb one thin finger through Olivia's hair and say that everything was going to be alright . . .

Olivia pried herself off of the squishy moss. A pop of pink had caught her attention. From behind the tree trunk, a copihue flower poked out its bright little head. Olivia's eyes widened, the peaceful warmth fresh in her mind. *Just one, or maybe two, more.* She really needed it right now.

Olivia snatched as many flowers as she could fit in her fist and threw them into her mouth. She swallowed before she could finish chewing, anxious to feel its heat melt away her sadness.

Nothing happened.

It had been almost instant before, but still, Olivia felt nothing. She stared at the remaining pink flowers blooming out of the short green bush. *This is the same plant, isn't it?* She bent to inspect it closer. It definitely didn't seem as viney as she remembered, and the shape of the flower was less like a bell and more like a very round woman squeezing herself into a dress three sizes too small.

No. It wasn't the same plant, not at all. *How could I be so stupid?*

Olivia coughed, but nothing but dry air came out. She needed water, now. Sprinting toward the sound of the river, she barreled through the dense thicket of ferns and bushes, not caring how many twigs ripped into her jacket. Finally, she reached the shore. Throwing herself to her knees, she splashed as much water into her mouth as she could. She swished and spit, rinsed and repeated, trying to clean herself of whatever it was she had eaten.

Nothing more she could do, Olivia lay back against a nearby tree and looked at the sky, praying, *please don't be poisonous, please don't be poisonous.*

Up above, the puffy white clouds remained still, but the patches of blue floated by like a river. *How can that be?* Olivia dropped her gaze to the actual river in front of her, searching for an explanation. Its glittering surface wasn't moving downstream as it should be, but expanding outward and contracting inward, like the water was breathing. With each rippling pulse, it shifted colors from turquoise to lavender to coral pink.

Olivia clawed at her hair. This couldn't be real. Maybe her fall had been harder than she thought, and maybe she was asleep in a hospital bed, waiting to wake up. That was it. She only had to wake up. *Wake up. Wake UP!*

When Olivia opened her eyes, she wasn't in the hospital as she had hoped. She was still in the forest, and things were worse than before. Everything around her was vibrating and brimming with color and light. The neon leaves danced in swoops and swirls. The lines of the knotted tree bark spiraled round, coiling inward before wriggling into the nearest branch.

"Hoooooo-woo!" came a loud yell.

Olivia knew instantly what that was: her father's call. But it couldn't be. She wobbled to her feet, clinging to the still-pulsating tree behind her. She peeked around, searching for a ghost.

In a flash, Max shot past her, leaving a trail of rainbow-colored light. Olivia jolted into action, sprinting after him. She followed his neon trail until she reached a small clearing in the trees. There he waited, as happy as can be. Olivia ran to embrace him, but her arms went straight through him.

"Good boy, Max!"

There was no mistaking that voice. Olivia turned, and there he was. With his fiery-red hair blazing brighter than she'd ever seen and his blue eyes glittering like diamonds, Olivia's father stood before her.

Olivia knew this wasn't real, but she was sure it wasn't a dream either. Which meant that flower she had eaten must be causing her to see things. That was the only reasonable explanation.

"Come on!" Her father waved her forward.

It's not real, it's not real, Olivia told herself as her eyes filled with tears. Even though she knew this at her core, the vision before her was so much more vivid than any dream she'd ever had. She couldn't resist reaching out to touch him. But before she could take two steps forward, another cold wind passed through her.

Amanda, Monica, Jill, and Emma ran up beside her, all of them wearing their Scout uniforms. Jill's mom walked out last, wearing her navy blue scout leader vest and carrying a big backpack stuffed to the brim. The girls formed a semicircle around Olivia's dad, eagerly awaiting to hear what he had to say.

"Today we're going to learn a very important lesson that could one day save your life." Her dad looked at the girls one by one, making sure he had their undivided attention. When he got to Olivia, he gave a quick wink before continuing. "Does anyone know, if you ever get lost in the woods and don't know which way you're walking, how can you find north?"

Jill shot her hand in the air. Olivia couldn't help but smile. She was such a know-it-all. Her dad pointed to Jill, and she answered, "Use a compass!"

"Yes, compasses are great, but what if you don't have a compass?"

Jill's face dropped. She didn't have an answer.

"No one knows? Okay, no worries. I'll show you."

Her dad picked up a tall stick from the ground. Max perked up his head, eyes wide.

"Sorry, bud, it's not for you." Her dad drove the stick into the ground. He then picked up a pebble and placed it at the top of the stick's skinny shadow. Olivia studied the ground in front of her. It was still blinking with color, but at least it wasn't vibrating much anymore. Imitating her father's actions, she found her own stick and stuck it into the ground.

"The sun sets in which direction?" Her dad asked the girls. "West!" yelled Jill before anyone else had a chance to answer.

"Remember to raise your hand, sweetie," called out Jill's mom, at which Jill rolled her eyes.

"That's okay. West is correct," Olivia's dad answered. Jill beamed with pride once more. He went on. "So if the sun is moving west, then the stick's shadow is moving—"

The girls were silent. Not even Jill knew this one.

Olivia's dad pulled a flashlight out of his pocket. He turned it on and shined it on the stick.

"The flashlight is the sun. So let's move it west." He walked left. The stick's shadow moved in the opposite direction.

Olivia now understood. What she needed to do next was simply wait for the shadow to move. She sat, resting her back against a tree. Everything seemed calmer now, still vibrating slightly but in a softer, more fluid way. Knowing that this vision could fade away at any moment, she happily watched her former self and the other girls run through the forest gathering dry bits of wood. They threw it all into a pile, the smaller pieces on the inside and the larger pieces forming a pyramid around them. Her dad then lit a match and within a few minutes, a small fire had started.

Olivia wished she could stay trapped in this memory forever, watching herself sitting by the fire, smiling and laughing and blissfully unaware of what was to come. But she knew she couldn't. The vision was already starting to fade. It was time to move on. She closed her eyes and inhaled deeply. When she opened them, everyone was gone.

Trying to ignore the sharp pain in her chest, Olivia got up to inspect her stick's shadow. It had moved substantially. She knew what she had to do next. Grabbing another pebble, she placed it on the shadow's new location. She then drew an *E* for east above this new stone, where the shadow had ended up. She turned to her left and drew a *W* above the first stone. She then drew a line connecting the two stones from west to east. The last step was to draw a perpendicular line through the middle of this line. At the top, she drew an *N*.

Olivia looked up. Forward was north.

Now there was only one thing left to do. She unwrapped Abu's scarf from around her neck. It was still damp and already starting to fall apart after receiving several slashes from the forest's many thorns. Feeling the tiniest bit of remorse for the sad crumpled scarf, Olivia began to tug at its seams. Soon she had unraveled a long strand of wool. She bit it off and wrapped multiple loops around a nearby tree branch.

Standing back, she admired what a good path-marker it made. The pink yarn was so hideously neon that it was impossible to miss against the sea of green leaves. *Perfect!* She wouldn't have any trouble finding her way back. Olivia laughed to herself. Apparently, her grandmother had made the right color choice after all.

"Thanks, Abu," Olivia whispered. "And thanks, Dad."

6.
STORM OF SADNESS

THE FARTHER OLIVIA walked into the depths of the forest, the stronger her feeling of loneliness. She tried to ignore it, focusing instead on marking her path and making sure each footstep kept straight north. A little bit farther. A few more steps. A few more skinny trees to wrap in pink yarn. After pushing past a million thorny bushes, she emerged into a clearing.

Olivia scanned the horizon. In front of her, the land dipped into a valley. There weren't trees for at least a mile, nothing but rocks and dirt and sun-bleached driftwood. Perhaps years ago this area had once been filled by a lake, but it was now bone dry. *What happened to the water?* Olivia reminded herself to focus on the real question: *Where is Max?* Had the owl really seen him come this way? And why in the world was she listening to an owl in the first place?

The fourth and final time Olivia scanned the horizon, her eyes stopped on a white triangle poking out above the treetops in the distance. *The volcano.* She was finally seeing it with her own eyes, not just in a photo. But it looked so far away. Max couldn't possibly have gone that far.

"Max?" Olivia called softly.

The sun slowly dipped down below the mountains, painting everything a heavenly, fluorescent-orange glow. As the sun dropped, so did the temperature. Olivia's hands were shaking as was her body, but she wasn't sure if that was from the cold. The loneliness and despair she had tried to suppress were now bubbling inside of her, impossible to ignore. Giving up, she allowed her body to crumble to the ground. Throwing her head back into the air, she released the loudest, most violent scream that she'd been holding inside herself for months.

A huge flock of birds shot out of the forest, dotting the sky black. They raced out over the canyon before making a sharp turn back. Olivia dodged behind the nearest tree. Tucu had warned her about a swarm of black things. Holding her breath, she peeked out. Only after the last wing flew out of sight did she exhale.

Olivia slumped against the tree as tears welled in her eyes. *Get up,* she thought. *Don't be the damsel in distress.* Her dad had always told her this when she was feeling sad.

"You want to wait around to get rescued?" he would ask. "Or do you want to look for a solution yourself? Don't be the damsel in distress. Be the hero!"

Olivia rocked back and forth, repeating in her head, *Be the hero, be the hero, be the hero.* But she wasn't the hero. She had failed. Not only had she not found Max, but she wasn't even sure if she would be able to find her own way out of this forest.

Her vision blurred as her eyelids filled. She wiped away as much as she could, but it was too late. As soon as the first tear broke free, the dam was broken.

As she felt the flood wash over her face, Olivia recalled the one other time that she had lost her dog. It was the day that she had received the worst news ever. Olivia could only recall certain words that bounced around inside her head over and over again. Words like "*stage four*" and "*20 percent chance of recovery.*" Once her dad had finished talking, they sat in silence. Olivia hadn't been able to speak. Because if she had acknowledged what her father had said, then it would become true.

But *it can't be true,* she had thought as she had fled her house.

Her bare feet had sprinted the length of their cobblestone driveway, down the hot asphalt road, across the busy street, up the wooden boardwalk, through the sand, all the way to the edge of the ocean. She had thrown herself into the wet sand and let the tide roll over her legs.

Olivia had cried so hard that day that she hadn't noticed that Max had run the entire way with her—because of course he had—nor that a storm was sneaking up on them. Olivia remembered it now as if it were yesterday. Lightning had lit up the sky, each flash followed by a boom of thunder. She could perfectly picture the look of sheer terror that had come over Max's face—his eyes wide, his ears flat against his head, his body lowered and trembling. He had only lasted thirty seconds until the third round of thunder struck. Then he was gone.

But unlike now, Olivia hadn't been alone that day. Her parents had run after her and helped her search for Max for over an hour, unbothered by the pouring rain. Eventually, they had found him whimpering under their neighbor Miss Jane's car. They had taken him home, and after drying off, they all snuggled under the ugly pink and purple blanket Abu had crocheted, drinking chocolate submarines, and watching Olivia's favorite superhero movie, *The White Wolf.*

But no one was coming to rescue her now.

She was alone. And this time, Max might be lost for good.

Feeling drained of every last tear, Olivia lifted her head from her hands. She gasped. Everything she had pictured in her head about that day at the beach, it was real, and it was happening now. The sky had turned dark gray, releasing torrents of rain. A fierce wind sent her hair flying across her face. Every few seconds, a bolt of lightning flashed, lighting up the sky.

How had she not noticed a full-fledged storm forming all around her? What's more, how had the dry valley filled with so much water that it had turned into a raging river?

"Olivia!" she heard yelled from across the water. Olivia pushed back the wet hair stuck to her forehead and squinted. She thought she saw—

"Max?" she called. Through the rain, she could barely make out a dark silhouette. It appeared to be about Max's size.

"Olivia, wait there. I'm coming over!" yelled the same voice. It was coming from the silhouetted figure, who she now saw was indeed Max, but that didn't make sense. *Max can't speak.* Maybe she was still under the hypnotic effects of the flower, seeing and hearing things that weren't there.

As soon as Olivia had decided that this must be another vision, Max waded into the river, attempting to swim across to her. Olivia tensed up. Vision or not, she couldn't sit back and do nothing.

"Stop! No! It's too dangerous!" Olivia yelled, but it was too late. Before she could say another word, his head went under the water, and he was gone.

"Max!" Olivia screamed.

She quickly slid down the rocky terrain and dove in after him. The furious waves immediately pulled her under just as they had done to Max. She was dragged downstream, somersaulting underwater, crashing into the riverbed. Somehow managing to stabilize herself, she planted her feet and propelled herself out of the water. Inhaling a thirsty gulp of air, she desperately looked for her dog. It was difficult to see anything as the rain fell hard and the river jolted her up and down. A bolt of lightning illuminated the landscape. Olivia scanned the area, yet she couldn't see Max.

As Olivia opened her mouth to scream his name once more, she plunged downward. After a few seconds, she re-emerged, coughing up water. New plan. Survival had to be her only focus. She needed to get out of the water before it killed her.

"Olivia!" Another voice called from somewhere in the distance. Olivia turned her head as another wave swept her under. She twisted around underwater before the current mercifully spit her out once more. She searched desperately for the voice. *Diego?* He was running along the shore, attempting to keep up with her. She couldn't understand what he was saying over the sound of the rushing water, but he was motioning ahead.

Downstream there was a large fallen tree hanging out over the water.

This was it. This was her one chance.

Olivia raised her arms, preparing to grab hold, but as she came closer it became clear that the tree was too high. She would be swept right under it. She looked back toward Diego. He was dodging in and out of the trees, struggling to keep up with the speed of the water.

The tree trunk got closer and closer. Too close. Diego wasn't going to make it in time. She still had to try. Olivia had an idea, but she would only have one shot. She took a big breath, closed her eyes, and bent her knees against her body, letting herself sink underwater. Praying it wasn't too deep, she shot her legs down hard and fast. Her feet contacted the rocky riverbed, and she pushed down with all her might, shooting herself upward. As she burst out of the water, she threw her arms as high as she could. Feeling a hard pressure on her wrist, she looked up. Diego was holding on to her.

But there was no time to rejoice. The stormy water continued to rush past Olivia on all sides as Diego clung to her, his eyes scrunched, and his teeth gritted. Above his head, a large bird circled them. It struggled against the strong wind before diving out of sight. *Was that...?* Diego's hand slipped and Olivia sunk a few inches into the water. He tried to pull her up, but the rushing water weighed her down. She was too heavy to lift. Olivia realized that her only hope was for Diego to hold on until the storm calmed, however long that may be.

As Diego's grip slipped once more, a huge four-legged figure appeared at the far end of the trunk. Its eyes were fixated on them, shining emerald green with each burst of lightning. It lurked forward. The wind and rain had no effect on this creature. His long claws plunged into the log, anchoring him firmly. Noticing the fear in Olivia's eyes, Diego twisted his head backward. His grip loosened, and Olivia slipped once more, water now up to her chin.

As the beast came closer, Olivia saw it—a puma. She didn't know much about this particular animal, but she knew it was a carnivore. The puma took one last step forward, now towering over them. Diego's hand trembled. He wouldn't be able to hold on much longer.

The puma looked at Olivia and for some reason, his eyes softened. He lowered his body against the tree trunk, dug his claws deep into its bark and began twisting down its side. He was so close now that Olivia could feel his breath on her face. As he opened his jaw, she closed her eyes, preparing to feel his teeth sink into her neck. Instead, something tugged on the collar of her jacket and, before she knew it, she was pulled out of the water.

She landed on something much softer than the rough tree trunk—the puma's back. She then witnessed the puma scooping up Diego with incredible ease and throwing him onto his back as well. Twisting around, he ran the length of the tree and leapt to shore.

Once they reached dry land, Olivia threw herself off the puma's back. The wind blew her hair into her face, blinding her. She clawed it out of her eyes, searching for a place to hide.

"Cub, you have nothing to fear," said the puma. "I am not going to hurt you." He lowered himself so that Diego could dismount, before shaking the water from his thick coat of fur.

Now that Olivia could see him up close, he seemed even more massive than before. He was at least seven feet long and three feet tall, even bigger than Lilli and Eli's Saint Bernard dog Igor. But unlike Igor's round fluffy body, the puma was sleek and muscular. He took a step forward. Olivia lurched backward.

"Please, don't come any closer," she whimpered.

"Very well." The puma sat and lowered his head to her. "But you must calm yourself now."

"What are you? Why? What?" Olivia's heart was beating fast and loud, and her breathing quickened. She was scared, anxious, and confused, but who wouldn't be after the day she had?

"You must trust me," said the puma. "If you do not calm yourself, this storm will never end."

"I think you should listen to him, Olivia," said Diego. Olivia's frown grew even deeper. What was he saying? And now Diego was speaking fluent English? "You would have drowned without him. I think we should trust him."

The puma tilted his head to Diego and blinked his green eyes slowly. He turned back to Olivia. "Listen to me, and do as I say. Close your eyes, and breathe deeply. Try to imagine a small fire building inside of you. Focus on that as hard as you can."

Olivia looked back and forth between Diego and the wild cat. They both sounded insane. But, they did seem like they wanted to help, and, to be honest, they were all she had right now. Out of options, she nodded. Closing her eyes, she inhaled a long deep breath. Heavy footsteps approached. Olivia could feel the puma's hot breath on her face, but for some reason, she wasn't frightened this time. The heat radiating from his body soothed her. Unconsciously, she began to match his breathing, her chest rising and falling to the same slow rhythm as his.

As Olivia continued to inhale and exhale, she felt the warm fire building inside her chest, just like he had described. It was similar to eating the copihue flower, but even more intense. Like a campfire crackling to life, it sizzled and popped, bathing her in the scent of musky smoke mixed with pine. The longer she focused on the fire, the more it overpowered the fear and sadness she had felt before.

When she opened her eyes, an orange ray of sunlight had appeared between the clouds. The rain slowed to a drizzle, and the distant rays of lightning appeared only as a dying echo of what they once were.

"It's working!" shouted Diego. "You're doing it!"

"But how?" asked Olivia. "How am I doing this?"

"Your emotions are stronger than you know," said the puma.

What's with all these animals and their cryptic messages? Olivia couldn't begin to understand any of what was happening, but now that she was calm, she remembered why she was here in the first place. "Max! I saw him."

"Which way did he go?" asked Diego. "We can still find him!"

Thinking of Max's face before he went underwater, Olivia's stomach clenched. "He was swept away. I don't even know if—" she stopped herself and took another deep breath.

"I did see a strange-looking creature float by in the water," replied the puma. "Perhaps it was him."

"You saw him? Was he okay?"

"He was struggling, but he was alive," said the puma. "Is he your friend?"

"He's my family! I need to find him and go home as soon as possible."

"I'll help you, Olivia!" said Diego.

The puma tilted his head, squinting at Diego and Olivia for a few seconds. He nodded. "It appears Tucu was right about you. Yes, you should be reunited with your family. Come with me. I will take you somewhere safe, and tomorrow we will see who else has seen your dog."

With that, the puma turned and prowled ahead.

"Tomorrow?" asked Olivia. "I need to find him now!"

"It is too dark to search for him now," replied the puma, without looking back. "And you need to rest."

It was true that there remained only a sliver of sunlight left. In no time at all it would be pitch black. Although Olivia was desperate to find Max and was not exactly sure why this puma was interested in helping her, she had no other choice but to trust him—for now. She looked at Diego and nodded, and the two of them began to follow the puma through the forest.

7.

HIGHWAYS OF LIGHT

SKILLFULLY ZIG-ZAGGING AROUND the tall, moss-covered trees, the puma led the way through the forest. The children struggled to keep up, not nearly as nimble as their feline companion. As they pushed past ferns and ducked under low-hanging branches, Olivia glanced at Diego. She could barely see, but she thought she saw a smile.

"*Pssst!* Diego!" Olivia whispered, still not fully trusting the puma. "How did you find me here?"

"Oh, well, when you didn't return, don Pancho and I went looking for you. He's really worried!"

Olivia's stomach sank. *Ma must be worried too.* And now that she was going to be spending the night here, she couldn't even imagine Ma's anxiety.

"We were about to go back and call the police, but then I heard your voice," said Diego. "It sounded like it was coming from under that huge alerce tree. I thought maybe you were stuck or something, so I crawled in and . . . oh man, I thought I was going to die! I was all *AHHHH* and then SPLASH!" Diego's hand gestures were even more expressive than his words. "Well, you must know since you went through too. Anyways, when I came out into this forest, I saw a tree with pink wool wrapped around it. I knew it was from your scarf, so I followed it until I found you!"

"What about Tata . . . I mean, don Pancho? Why didn't he come too?"

"Oh, well, I heard those roots start to move around behind me. I guess he didn't make it through in time." Diego shrugged like he wasn't at all concerned about this.

"Hey, did you know about this place? The, uh, strangeness?" Olivia asked, eyebrow raised.

"Oh, well, don Pancho says a lot of crazy things about the forest. That it has *secrets.*"

"And demons, like the trauco?" Olivia gulped.

"The trauco? Oh, no, he can't leave the island of Chiloé!" Diego chuckled. "Just kidding. That's only a myth the old ladies like to talk about. Don Pancho says it's not true, but he's told me other things. I always assumed that—" His voice trailed off, and his smile grew from ear to ear. "Oh man! He's not going to believe this! He was right! Hey Mr. Puma, after this, would you mind visiting an old friend? Just to prove he was right. Pretty please?" Diego grinned.

The large cat looked back at him silently.

"No? Not a chance?" asked Diego, still grinning. "Well, will you tell us your name at least?"

"Newen," replied the puma without looking back.

"Newen! Cool name," said Diego. "I'm Diego, and she's Olivia."

The puma turned and nodded in acknowledgment. Olivia's eyes grew wide. It was the most majestic greeting she had ever received.

"Hey, wait." Olivia frowned. "Diego, how is it that you're speaking English so well now?"

"What are you talking about?" Diego laughed. "I'm not speaking English. You're speaking Spanish!"

"What?" Olivia shook her head. "Nothing makes any sense here."

To this, the puma replied, "Just because you don't understand something does not mean it doesn't make sense." He stopped in his tracks. "Look at this tree. What do you see?"

Olivia approached the tree to study it. At first glance, it looked like any other ordinary tree, but the longer she focused on it the clearer it became. This late into the evening, the tree should appear as dark as a shadow, but it didn't. It was as if it had a faint glow to it, like the roots in that tunnel. Olivia took another step forward, her eyes wide. She brought her face closer to the tree until it was mere inches away. The glowing light was moving in little dotted highways. Her eyes followed the light speeding into the diverging branches and back down into the roots.

"Wow! What is that?" asked Diego.

Olivia had been so enthralled in the light that she hadn't noticed him standing beside her.

"It has many names," replied Newen. "The elders call it Ngünemapun, but most of us refer to it simply as the Energy. It flows through every living thing, both plant and animal, connecting us all. This light you see passing through the trees is like a network, allowing them to communicate with each other."

Olivia was bewildered. *Trees talking to each other?* She grabbed hold of a small branch to her left and pressed her ear against the cold bark. In a crack, the branch broke off in her hand. The tree's white lights turned red. Before she could step backward, the forest filled with the same mysterious whispers from before. Now all the trees were glowing red.

"They have spoken," said Newen. "Announcing the presence of a potential threat."

"Who? Me?" asked Olivia, looking at the branch in her hand. "No, I'm not a threat! Can you, like, tell them that?"

Newen approached the same tree and rubbed his back across its trunk. The trees' red lights faded back to white, and the whispers died down.

So, it had been the trees whispering this whole time! One mystery solved. But Olivia was still left with too many questions to count. "How did you do that? And wait, how can you and I communicate? And how are Diego and I speaking the same language now? And how—"

"Look at your own skin," answered Newen.

Olivia raised her hands and squinted. There it was. The same glowing energy was within her. She pushed back her right jacket sleeve and followed the light up her arm. Also busy inspecting his skin, Diego pulled up his sweater and puffed out his stomach, watching it glow in amazement. Olivia noticed the light wasn't only contained within their skin. It looked like Diego had spouted tiny white roots from his feet, which then expanded out, connecting with the glowing roots emerging from her own feet. And Newen. And the trees. They were all connected by these faint trails of light.

"Cool!" said Diego, waving his hand around as if he were holding a glow stick. "Why doesn't this light or, uh, Energy, exist back home?"

"It once did." Newen walked a few paces forward and stopped in front of a different tree. This one wasn't shining at all and appeared as black as coal. "The Energy is fragile. It is passed between every living thing, but the trees have always been the strongest carriers. Their roots travel long distances underground, carrying the Energy from one to another. But if one tree falls, it causes a break in the connection. The Energy must immediately find a new path, a new tree, to connect to. If too many trees die, the Energy disappears."

Thinking of her grandfather yelling at the loggers, Olivia now understood why he had been so angry. By cutting down a mere handful of trees, the loggers were affecting the entire forest. She clenched her fist. It was their own fault that this Energy, this beautiful light, no longer existed in the human world. They had been too careless, caused too much destruction. She held out her hand and touched the dark, lifeless tree. It didn't change colors or react at all.

"Wait! If there are no humans here, then what happened to this tree?" Olivia asked. "Why did it die?"

"This tree has a sister on the other side," replied Newen. "It cannot survive without her."

The puma didn't need to explain further. Olivia understood. The human's actions not only had consequences in their own forest but in this *other* forest as well. Even though she knew she wasn't personally responsible for any of this, she felt an intense pang of guilt.

"Come," said Newen. "We're almost there."

8.
Human Cubs

A LARGE ROCK wall appeared ahead, slanting inward in the middle, not quite deep enough to form a cave, but enough to protect from the rain and predators. The rock looked as though someone had cut it into large slabs and stacked them together diagonally, creating a jagged patchwork quilt of bluish-grays and rusty-oranges.

As Olivia studied the rock formation, a three-legged fox popped out and hopped straight over to them.

"Newen, you're back!" The little fox cocked her head sideways, eyeing the two humans. "You've brought our dinner back alive, have you?"

Olivia tensed up. *So this really is a trap!*

"Ha!" Squeaked the fox. "I'm just playing."

Olivia exhaled. A three-legged jokester fox. *Of course. What's next? A juggling bear?*

"Who have you brought Newen?" asked the fox.

"They are cubs I found in the storm," Newen responded. "Tucu told me of their arrival. They are in need of our protection."

"Oh, of course! Welcome, little cubs!" The vixen hopped over on her three legs and rubbed her head on Olivia's knees and then Diego's. "My name is Ruda."

She was smaller and much less orange than what Olivia had always imagined a fox would look like in real life. She was about the size of Jill's cat Boots and even had the same big bushy tail that ended in a black tip. Her body was slim, and her fur speckled gray and white, with a few splashes of orange on her legs, ears, and snout.

Diego knelt and reached a hand out. "Hi Ruda! I'm Diego and she's Olivia. It's very nice to meet you."

Sniffing Diego's outstretched hand, Ruda cocked her head, her whiskers twitching.

"Say, Newen, what type of cubs are they exactly?" She continued to scan every inch of Diego's hand with her nose. "They don't smell like any animal I know."

"They are human cubs, Ruda," replied Newen.

Ruda straightened her body, rigid, before skirting away. "That's not possible. How did they get here?"

"Why don't you ask them?" said Newen.

Ruda hopped over to Olivia, head lowered. "How did you get here, human cub?"

Olivia glanced at Diego, confused, then back at the fox. "Well, we sort of, uh, fell in through that huge tree."

"The alerce tree!" Diego pitched in. "What's the big deal? You've really never seen humans before?"

"Newen, you know what this means?" Ruda eyed the puma, who was busy licking himself clean. "Well, fine. They're here now, somehow. Sit. Tell us who you are and why you're here."

"Okay!" Diego skipped over and plopped himself down next to the little fox as if he had known her his entire life. "Like I said, my name is Diego, and I'm eleven and a half years old. I've lived here in Lenca my *whooooole* life! Not like Olivia. She came all the way from the United States!"

"Where's the *Oonaytay Stays*?" asked Ruda. "Is that north or south of the volcano?"

"Uh . . . way, way north," answered Olivia.

"You flew here on a plane, didn't you?" asked Diego, eyes wide.

"Yeah, of course," Olivia shrugged.

"That's so cool! I hope I get to fly on a plane one day," he said.

"What's a plane? Is it a bird?" asked Ruda.

"Sort of!" replied Diego. "But like huge metal birds that carry thousands of people all over the world! *Shooowoosh!*" He made a soaring movement with his right arm.

Ruda scrunched up the orange fur on her snout. "Birds that carry *humans*? I've never heard of such a thing." She turned to Olivia. "And you rode one of these birds here?"

"Uh, yes," replied Olivia, wrapping her arms around herself. She had only just realized she was shivering. Clothes still wet from her wild river ride, she removed her jacket and twisted it tight to wring the water out.

"Why did you risk such a dangerous journey?" asked Ruda.

"Oh, well, my grandparents live here." Olivia's stomach tensed as she remembered how worried they must be. "And my mother wanted to be closer to them." This wasn't a lie as much as a half truth.

Diego cleared his throat. "Didn't . . . uh . . . didn't your dad die?"

Olivia froze, her left shoe half off. How did he know that? The one and only advantage of moving to the opposite end of the world was that nobody was supposed to know anything about what happened. Or at least they weren't supposed to talk about it.

"Yes," she replied softly, pretending to fuss with her shoelaces.

"Oh, I'm sorry." Ruda lowered her head. "Was he eaten?"

"Eaten?" Olivia frowned.

"No? Starved then? Not strong enough to hunt?"

"What? No!" Oliva slammed her right shoe on the ground.

Diego suppressed a giggle with both hands before composing himself. "He got sick with cancer, right? That's what don Pancho said. He said you'd be sad so I should be extra nice to you. But you don't seem all that sad."

"I prefer not to talk about it," said Olivia, still refusing to meet his gaze.

"You should beware the cage of your own creation," said Newen. And just like that, he went back to slathering saliva down the length of his forearm.

Olivia glared at the puma. He sounded like Tucu with his "*darkness within*" comment. She didn't know what either of them were talking about or why they were pretending to know anything about her life. Annoyed, she shifted her eyes to where a small pile of dry twigs lay on the ground. *Perfect.*

Olivia walked over to begin collecting as many sticks as she could. They may be enough to start a fire, or, at the very least, they would distract her from this annoying conversation.

"What are you doing, building a nest?" asked Ruda, hopping closer.

"No, I'm going to make a fire," Olivia responded.

The fox flattened her ears against her head exactly like Max did when he was scared. Newen paused his bath to give Olivia a stern look.

"Newen!" Ruda sprinted over to the puma and pounced on his back. "Stop her! She's going to burn down our home!"

"What? No, no!" said Olivia. "I know how to control it. It won't burn anything besides these sticks." She held out the bundle as evidence, hoping it would be enough to calm the frantic fox. It didn't seem to work.

"Are you sure you know how to control it?" asked Newen.

"Yes, I promise," replied Olivia. "As long as it's surrounded by nothing but rocks and dirt, it won't go anywhere." She waited, still holding out the dry twigs. A shiver ran up her neck. "I'm just cold."

Newen nodded. Ruda frowned, still not at all convinced, but Olivia took it that Newen's permission was all she needed. As Olivia broke apart the smallest twigs to make a tinder nest, Diego scooted closer.

"You really know how to start it without matches?" he asked.

"Yes," said Olivia curtly. This wasn't entirely true, as the only time she'd done it successfully she'd had a lot of help, but she wasn't about to mention this, as she was still annoyed with Diego for mentioning her dad in the first place.

"Hey, if you want to help, maybe you could look for some berries to eat or something."

"On it!" Diego sprung to action.

Olivia had little hope of Diego finding anything edible, but now that she was free from his prying questions, she could focus on her task in peace. Once she'd finished separating two piles of sticks, one for tinder and one with bigger pieces to build a pyre, it was time for the hardest part—creating enough friction to ignite a spark. This was the most difficult method of starting a fire, much harder than using a magnifying glass. But as there was no sun or glass, it was her only option. Placing the flattest stick she could find on the ground, she carved a notch in it with a sharp rock. Now there was only one thing left to do. She took a deep breath and looked up. Ruda and Newen were watching her closely.

"Wish me luck," Olivia said.

Neither animal said anything, apart from a small scoff from Ruda.

Placing a tall stick in the notch, Olivia began to spin the spindle between her palms, applying as much pressure as she could to drive it down. Theoretically, this should be enough to create a small ember for the fire. After a couple minutes, however, the only things burning were Olivia's hands. Stopping to collect her breath, she spit into her raw palms, rubbed them together, and then inspected the notch. It was a little deeper, but there was still no sign of smoke. Olivia exhaled, already exhausted.

"I would like to help," Newen announced. He took two steps toward the little pile of sticks and nodded, which Olivia assumed meant she should continue. Unsure how his presence would be any help, she shrugged and continued spinning the stick. As she did so, Newen lowered his head. He closed his eyes and exhaled, his breath sending a cloud of dust into the air. The dust then turned into smoke, from where a small red ember appeared. Olivia's eyes widened.

Snapping out of her state of awe, she swiftly carried the smoking piece of wood over to her pile of tinder and patted it until the ember fell on top.

"How did you do that?" asked Olivia, as she continued to blow on the tiny ember struggling to survive.

"The Energy can transmit more than words," said Newen. "If our feelings are strong enough, it will find a way to manifest them as well. All I had to do to create this fire was focus on feeling warm and calm."

With one last breath, the orange ember burst to life, igniting the small tinder nest. Olivia quickly added bigger pieces of wood. As she watched the small fire's flickering dance, she wondered. During the storm, Newen had told her to calm herself by breathing deeply and imagining a small fire burning inside of herself. It had worked then. She imitated Newen's actions, closing her eyes and inhaling a long deep breath. She imagined the fire in her chest. The bright yellows, oranges, and reds. The soft hissing and crackling. The smell of smoke and pine and dirt mixed together. A marshmallow melting on a stick. Her friends laughing. Telling ghost stories by flashlight.

"Impressive," said Ruda.

Olivia opened her eyes. The fire was much taller.

"You have an incredible gift," Newen said.

"I want to try!" Diego had returned and dumped a pile of midnight blue berries at his feet. He shut his eyes and clenched his fists, scrunching up his face in concentration. After a mere five seconds, he peeked open an eye. The fire hadn't changed at all.

"No fair," he groaned, plopping himself on the ground.

"Not everyone can do this without proper training," said Newen. "It takes a great deal of focus and a very pure emotion." He locked eyes with Olivia. "You must be careful and learn to control it before it controls you."

Olivia nodded, although she wasn't quite sure how *it* could control *her*. Sitting back down, she grabbed a handful of berries. She hesitated before tossing them back.

"Diego, these berries, what, uh—"

"They're *maqui* berries!" he grinned, his tongue already painted blue. "Kind of like blueberries, but with a crunchy seed in the middle. Don Pancho says they're a super fruit!"

Olivia nodded. Now satisfied that she wasn't about to eat another questionable, mind-bending plant, she gulped down the berries. They did indeed have a bit of an unpleasant crunch, but other than that, they were quite tasty, and she was truly starving. Wiping some blue slobber from her lips, she reached for another greedy handful.

When the pile of berries was down to its last few pieces, Olivia leaned back, satisfied. Stretching out her feet to warm them by the fire, she watched the others. Diego was busy explaining the concept of school to Ruda, whose ears were perked in interest. Newen, still not done with his bath, was now gnawing the insides of his toes. Olivia smirked. Of the many campfires she'd sat beside, she'd never experienced one quite like this. As she was about to close her eyes, she remembered Max. She whipped upright, burning with guilt. Here she was making friends while he was out there somewhere, scared and all alone.

"Ruda, have you seen a dog go by? He got dragged down the river in the storm."

"A dog? I've never even heard of such a creature," replied Ruda, head cocked. "Such strange things are happening in the forest lately. So called planes, and dogs, and even *humans* in the forest! Brumas everywhere. What's next? Is Kutral going to escape again?"

"Who's Kutral?" asked Diego.

"Oh, he's—" Ruda began.

"A sad, confused creature," interrupted Newen. "You don't need to worry about him." He glared at Ruda with his eyes full of warning before turning back

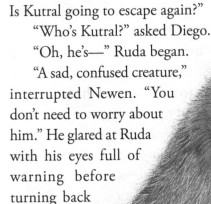

toward the children. "He lives far away, at the volcano."

"Lives there? More like trapped there." Ruda's wide eyes shined gold by the fire. "They say any creature who gets too close starts to hear voices and see visions until they go mad and throw themselves in. But nowadays you don't even have to go to the volcano to fall under his spell. If the Brumas catch you, well, they're just as bad."

The hair on the back of Olivia's neck stood on end.

"What are Brumas?" Diego asked, seeming more intrigued than concerned.

"More sad creatures," said Newen. "But now is not the time to worry about these things. We are safe here, and it is time to rest. When the sun rises, we will go looking for your dog."

This was the first time Olivia was hearing the word *Brumas*, but she had a feeling they were the dark flying things Tucu warned her about. In any case, it didn't seem like she was going to get any more information out of Newen tonight. Maybe it was best to leave it that way. She needed to find Max. Then they could leave before getting into any more trouble.

Newen stood, stretched his front paws, and paced over to the children. He circled around them twice, then lay down in a heap. Hopping over, Ruda nestled in under Newen's back leg, wearing his long tail as a blanket. Diego, as confident as ever, happily snuggled into Newen's chest.

The sun had set long ago, yet the night was glowing brighter each passing minute. The trees twinkled with light as if they had swallowed all the stars in the sky. Watching them glitter, Olivia tried to process everything that had happened that day. Although her body was physically exhausted, her mind was spinning.

After a little while, she let herself curl up with the others. Though she knew the small fire would soon die out, the bed of fur was so soft and warm that she didn't care. As she sank another inch into the puma's chest, she couldn't help but think of her own furry companion. Had Max found somewhere safe to sleep?

Let him know I'm here, Olivia thought. *And I'm coming for him.*

She exhaled long and heavy. She would find him. She had to. This was her promise to herself. With Max's face still etched in her mind, she closed her eyes and soon fell under the black blanket of sleep.

9.

TIQUE AND THE DALCA

SUNLIGHT FLOODED IN through the cracks in Olivia's eyelids. It was morning, but she was not in her bedroom—or any room. As she stretched her toes, the events of the day before flashed in her mind. It seemed like an impossible dream, but as her cheek rubbed against Newen's soft fur, she knew it was real.

Olivia breathed in the puma's scent as she allowed herself one more minute to snuggle into his delicious warmth. There wasn't even the slightest hint of chamomile shampoo, but something about him still reminded her of Max. Peeling herself away, she noticed two small eyes staring at her from behind a fern. They stood not a foot off the ground, but that was all she could make out of the animal's size, as the rest of it was lost in the shadows. In a blink, they were gone.

Before she could stand, something rough and slimy, like wet sandpaper, ran across Olivia's head. She jumped to her feet, startled. Newen let out a large yawn, revealing all the teeth at the back of his mouth. He then began licking himself all over, from his paw up to his forearm. He continued down his body until he reached Diego's sleeping head. Diego giggled half-consciously as Newen's long pink tongue ran across his hair, plastering it to his forehead.

Olivia tilted her head, watching the spectacle before her. Was Newen *cleaning* Diego? She felt the wet spot on her own head and smiled.

A pitter-patter of quick feet startled her. Ruda approached and released three spotted eggs from her mouth, depositing them onto a pile of huge green leaves, round tree nuts, pink flowers, and cream-colored mushrooms. Noticing Olivia watching her, the fox hopped twice in delight.

"Oh good, you're awake!" she piped. "I can't reach the maqui berries, and I didn't know what else human cubs eat, so I brought anything I could find."

"Oh, wow! Thank you." Olivia walked over to inspect the foraged food. These weren't exactly her normal breakfast choices. She swallowed hard.

She didn't dare eat any more flowers, not after what happened last time. And she feared the mushrooms and raw eggs would make her sick. Grabbing one of the nuts, she attempted to crack it open between her teeth, but its shell was as hard as a rock. Dropping the nut, she reached for her last option. The massive leaf looked like it was making a huge effort to not be eaten, as it was three times as big as her head, and its stalk was as round as her arm. Both were dotted with rough bumps that must make it extremely unpleasant to bite into. But Ruda was watching her so eagerly, and Olivia supposed it was the safest choice after all.

Olivia opened her mouth wide enough to take the smallest nibble.

"Olivia, stop." Diego stretched his arms in the air, letting out one big yawn. "We don't eat the leaf of the nalca. We eat this part."

He wobbled over and took the bumpy stalk from her. Placing it over his knee, he pressed down on both sides until it snapped in two. He handed her half and kept the other for himself. "Peel this back and eat the insides," he instructed.

Olivia watched first, then followed suit. Inside the rough green exterior was a slab of pinkish white meat. She took a cautious bite. It was crunchy and slightly acidic, like the absolute worst vegetable on earth—celery.

"Good, right?" Diego said with a mouth full of white mush.

Olivia hummed an "*mmhmm,*" resisting the urge to spit it out. Closing her eyes, she tried to imagine eating it with peanut butter, just like when forced to eat celery. She'd paint peanut butter on it, then she'd scoop out one more gigantic spoonful and plop that one on Max's nose. He'd be busy licking it off for ten minutes straight, making her laugh until her belly hurt. It was so funny that eating celery was *almost* bearable. But Olivia didn't have peanut butter—and she didn't have Max either. Opening her eyes, she forced herself to swallow.

Ruda cleared her throat. "Good, good! I assume that, since you only need your two back paws for walking, you can eat and walk at the same time, yes? I only need three paws, you know, but I'm afraid I wouldn't get very far on two."

Ruda stood tall on her two back paws and teetered toward Newen, who was still busy bathing every inch of himself. She made it halfway there before falling forward, catching herself gracefully with her one front paw.

"Newen, the cubs are fed and ready to move!" Ruda ran around, jumped over, and pushed into his back. "Come on, get up!"

Letting out another big yawn, Newen slowly raised his body off the ground. He pointed his backside high in the air as he stretched his front paws in front of him. "All right, Ruda, I'm up. And I know who to see."

"Great. Let's go!" Ruda dashed into the forest without looking back. After five seconds, she reappeared, hopping up and down. "Come on, come on!"

Olivia nibbled on her *nalca* stem as she followed Newen, Ruda, and Diego through the forest. They walked for ten minutes or so until arriving at a riverbank. Unlike the rapids from the day before, the water here drifted lazily. Approaching the edge of the riverbank, Newen and Ruda lowered their heads to lap up a few gulps of water.

It was then that Olivia realized how dry her mouth was. Her lips were beginning to crack, and her tongue felt fuzzy. It was as if this overwhelming thirst had snuck up on her out of nowhere. In Scouts, she had been taught not to drink unpurified water because of the dirt and bacteria, not to mention the more disgusting, unmentionable waste. But this water looked so crystal clear and pure, she couldn't resist. Olivia cupped her hands into the water. She brought it up to her face and slurped. It was even more delicious than Ma's famous chocolate submarines, somehow sweet and crisp and so very icy cold.

Plunging her hands into the water for a second helping, she noticed movement below the surface. A fish? As she leaned closer, a furry little face popped up. Olivia recoiled in shock. Diego gasped and clapped in glee.

"An otter!" He reached his hand toward it, sending the otter ducking back underwater. "Hey, wait! Come back."

The otter peeped his head back up, presenting a perfectly smooth pebble in its paw. He placed it on his tail and flicked it into the air. Giggling with glee, Diego jumped for it. Olivia chuckled, only now realizing the otter was playing catch.

As Diego tossed the pebble back into the river, Ruda spoke up. "Tique, we have a—"

The otter dove back under in search of the pebble. Ruda ruffled her nose impatiently as she waited for him to reappear. He was back after a few seconds, spiking the pebble toward Diego once more.

"Sorry to disturb your little game," continued Ruda, "but we have a rather important question for you."

"Fire away!" replied Tique the otter, managing to catch the pebble mid-air.

"Right," said Ruda, visibly annoyed at not having his undivided attention. "Well, first of all, you should meet Olivia and Diego. Olivia is looking for her dog, Max."

"What's a *dogmax*?" asked Tique.

There was a brief silence before Olivia remembered that none of the animals had ever seen a dog. "Oh, right! Well, he's about this tall and his fur is kind of an orangey-brown color with dark spots, and, um, he wears a green collar or . . . stripe . . . around his neck. Have you seen him?"

"Oh, yes! I've seen that dogmax," replied the otter as he continued to flit back and forth in the water. "He's not very good at swimming, no, not at all. He came crashing through here, twirling around this way and that. He managed to get out over there, but then some Brumas came flying through. I tried to tell him to hide, I did, but he didn't hear me. You can't outrun the Brumas. Everyone knows that. You know, I've never seen a dogmax before."

Olivia raised her eyebrows. There was that word again. *"Brumas?"*

"Yes, that's what I said, Brumas! Nasty things." The otter perched himself on a log, tilting his head at Newen and Ruda. "Where did you find this strange creature who has never seen a Bruma before?"

"They're human cubs!" said Ruda, twitching her fluffy eyebrows.

The otter plunged back underwater. A minute passed until Olivia found his little face peeking out behind a rock.

"What are you doing bringing human cubs here, Ruda? And you, Newen, how could you?"

"They arrived on their own," said Newen.

"I thought the entrance was closed years ago."

"It was, but something's caused it to open once more."

Tique looked from one child to the other and then back to Newen and Ruda, frowning.

"So, why are you helping them anyway? Boldo says that—"

"Who's—" Olivia began.

"Why are you listening to that crazy cat?" Ruda raised the hair on the back of her neck.

"Well, he says some interesting things, you know," Tique replied. "And he might be right. Even I know what humans are capable of!"

"What we're—" Olivia interjected once more.

"Tique, there is goodness in these cubs," said Newen. "They came all this way looking for their dog Max. They say he is their family."

Tique slowly emerged from behind the rock. "The humans consider an animal their family?"

"Yes, he's my family!" cried Olivia, finally able to get a full sentence in. "He's like a brother to me. Will you help me find him . . . please?"

The otter tilted his head to the side, measuring her up like Tucu and Ruda had, deciding whether or not she could be trusted. Having apparently reached a decision, he nodded.

"Very well," said Tique. "Follow me."

And just like that he took off, darting through the water with Newen wading in after him.

Before Olivia could take a step forward, something nudged her side. Diego gave her a wide-eyed look that needed no explanation. He couldn't swim.

Thankfully, Olivia wasn't the first one to speak up.

"Tique, do we absolutely *have* to swim there?" Ruda wrinkled her snout.

Tique twisted around and darted underwater, a second later bobbing up inches from the shore. "I forgot you foxes can't swim." He pulled up his massive tail, sprinkling Ruda with water. Olivia would have assumed this was an accident had it not been for the grin on his furry face.

"Foxes can *too* swim," Ruda spat as she shook the water from her fur. "But we prefer not to get wet!"

Tique lay on his back, patting his stomach and squeaking out what must have been a laugh. Olivia took advantage of this opportunity to clear her throat.

"You know what? We humans aren't the best swimmers either. Is there another way to get there, maybe?"

"Oh, you poor things! A life out of water is no life at all. Well, let's see . . . " The otter looped around in the river as he thought. "Oh, yes, that could work! If it's still there, that is. Only one way to know. Come on, this way!"

This time, he splashed onto shore, shook the water off his body and exceptionally long tail, and wobbled into the forest.

Keeping close to the shore, they followed behind Tique, who was noticeably slower on land than in water. Eventually they came upon what looked like a large fallen tree trunk cut right down the middle. Coming closer, however, Olivia saw that it was actually several long planks of wood that appeared to be sewn together with reeds and some strange gluey substance.

"What is this?" Olivia asked as she inspected the strange construction.

"Wow!" yelled Diego, running to the large chunk of wood. "I never thought I'd get to see one of these outside a textbook. Help me flip it over, will you?"

Olivia joined him, and together they gripped the bottom of the wood and pulled upward until it flipped over.

"Yes, it is! A dalca!" Diego ran his fingers along the side, inspecting it inside and out.

"A what?" asked Olivia.

"It's a canoe used by the Huilliches."

"The who?"

Diego chuckled. "I forgot you don't know anything about Chile. They're the indigenous people who live in this area. Part of the Mapuche community, the biggest group in the country. Surely you've heard of them?"

"Oh, right. Of course," Olivia lied, wondering how many different indigenous people existed around the world. The only ones she could ever remember were the Powhatans, because they lived in

Virginia and were Pocahontas' tribe, and the Sioux, because Mandy would never shut up about the fact that she was 6 percent Sioux.

"Good find, Tique," said Newen. "If the humans use the dalca, can you lead us to where you saw their dog?

"Yes, yes, that was my idea after all!" Tique rolled in the mud like a puppy in a puddle.

"Awesome!" Diego was already attempting to push the dalca into the water by himself, with no success. The harder he pushed, the more his feet sank into the mud below. He looked back at the others. "A little help?"

Kneeling, Olivia pressed into the side of the dalca with all her might. Newen lowered himself, pushing against the wood with his back. Though Tique continued to play in the mud and Ruda's only help was directing them with her tail, the three of them had enough combined strength to dislodge the massive piece of wood toward the water from the muddy riverbank.

The water was up to Olivia's ankles, but the dalca was still hitting the bottom. They needed to keep moving until it was completely afloat. With one last push, the dalca was free. It rocked back and forth gently, patiently waiting for its passengers to board.

"Don't be shy. In you go!" Tique was already swimming circles around the floating wood.

Diego went first. Grabbing the edge of the dalca, he pushed down hard and tried to jump in. The boat rocked downward, nearly flipping over. Diego splashed into the water in defeat.

Swimming next to the dalca, Newen motioned with his head for Diego to climb on his back. The boy grabbed a fistful of back fur, clumsily pulling and pushing until he managed to raise himself up. Although clearly uncomfortable, Newen didn't complain.

Olivia went next, managing to pull herself up a bit more gracefully than Diego. After the children were successfully aboard, Ruda swam over, climbed on top of Newen, and clawed at the side of the wooden canoe with her one front paw. Seeing that the fox couldn't quite pull herself over the edge, Olivia lowered her hand to Ruda, offering it as a stepping stool.

Ruda looked at the hand and frowned. "Thank you, but I think I can do it myself." She continued to claw at the edge of the dalca with her single front paw, going nowhere.

"Push with your back paws, Ruda!" Diego called out. "Big hop!" He made a hopping motion, causing the boat to wobble.

Ruda placed her front paw on Newen's back, lowered herself in a pounce position, and jumped upward with the incredible strength of her back paws. She landed between the two children and immediately shook the water from her fur.

"You're a great hopper, Ruda! I knew you could do it." Diego patted the little fox on her head. He then grabbed a long skinny stick laying in the dalca, placed it on the bottom of the river, and pushed off. "Let's go!"

Tique the otter darted through the water ahead of them, leading the way.

10.
BRUMAS

THE RIVER SOON spilled out into a small laguna surrounded by mountains. The tall gray cliffs were dotted with rows of evergreen trees that became more sparse the higher they rose. The group stayed close to shore, pushing the dalca through the shallows. Olivia peered into the water below. It reflected the green and gray hues from above. Below the surface, groups of silver fish sparkled past.

"Wow, trout!" Diego rejoiced.

Olivia thought of Tata's fishing rod leaning idly against the cabin wall. It would get so much more use here, where the fish swam by in schools. Thinking of Tata's frustration at their disappearance, she asked, "Will the animals ever return to our side of the forest?"

Tique scoffed. "*Your* side?"

"I mean. . . I mean the other side . . . you know what I mean!" Olivia looked from one animal to the next. None made eye contact with her. She landed back on Newen. If any of them were going to give her an honest answer, it would be him. The puma continued to paddle through the water without redirecting his gaze.

"To answer that, you need to understand why we left in the first place," he began, turning his head toward her. "A long time ago, there weren't two sides of the forest. The animals and the humans shared the forest, along with the Energy in it. There was an understanding between us."

"Until those *other* humans arrived," said Tique, zig-zagging through the water. "Different humans, bad humans! They blocked off our rivers with big sticks and stones. We otters kept telling them not to do that, but they didn't seem to understand us at all. It was like they couldn't feel the Energy. They didn't stop with the rivers, either. No, they didn't. They took whatever they wanted; they took—"

"Everything," said Ruda. "They tore down trees, burnt entire forests, and built their farms on our land. They started leaving big silver teeth hidden in the forest, waiting for us to step on them and close upon us." Ruda raised the small stump where her right front paw had once been. "That is how I lost my paw."

"Oh, Ruda! I'm so sorry," said Olivia. She instinctively reached out a hand to pet the fox as she would Max but reconsidered.

"Don't be. It's only a paw," said Ruda with a twitch of sadness before shaking it off. "Others lost much more."

"Oh, yes," said Tique. "I thank the river every day that all of my family made it here safely. Poor Newen lost his mother, you know? So sad, it was. And then everything that happened with—"

"That's enough," said Newen.

Olivia stared at the puma. So he had also lost a parent. Then he knew what it felt like, the terrible emptiness that somehow weighed so much.

"What happened to her?" asked Diego.

"Humans," responded Newen without further explanation.

"Oh, I'm so sorry," Diego whispered.

"You do not need to apologize. You are not responsible for what other humans have done." Newen's furry brows dipped inward.

"Unfortunately, not everyone understands that. Do you remember what we told you about Kutral?"

"Something about being very dangerous, trapped at the volcano, and making people go crazy." Diego nodded as if this was a completely normal thing to say.

"Yes. But, there's more to Kutral's story that we did not tell you," said Newen. Ruda shot Newen a look, raising an eyebrow. Newen continued.

"He wasn't always what he is today. He was once very kind. But like so many of us, he also suffered a terrible loss at the hands of the humans. Instead of mourning this loss, he only thought of revenge." Newen slowed his pace. He shook his head before paddling on through the water. "He began stalking the humans he believed responsible. He waited until they were asleep and vulnerable. Then he attacked. But he didn't stop there. He became obsessed with making all humans suffer as he had. And so, the humans began defending themselves, coming into the forest with weapons, hunting us. It was then that we knew we could no longer live together in peace. The decision was made to not only banish Kutral to the volcano, but also to split the forest into two separate sides, one for us and one for the humans."

"But how?" asked Olivia.

"When we all come together to focus on one thing, one desire, we're able to harness our full Energy. And there is one object that, if we plant that Energy inside it, can make our desires come true."

"The canelo berry!" said Tique.

"The *what* berry?" asked Olivia.

"Canelo trees used to cover this region," explained Ruda. "The elders considered them sacred. They said that they could hold the Energy better than anything else here. Whenever they needed something, they would make a wish upon a canelo berry and then plant it in the ground."

"Before the last sacred canelo tree died, we saved as many of its berries as we could. But over the years, their number shrank until only three berries remained."

"Of those three, we used two," said Newen. "One to create a barrier to trap Kutral at the volcano, and another to create a new, protected forest."

"Ever since then, we've been safe from the humans," said Ruda.

"And the humans from us," said Newen.

"But now, only one canelo berry remains," said Tique.

A heavy silence washed over them. As they continued drifting through the laguna, Olivia daydreamed about the canelo berry ceremony, imagining a whole forest of animals gathered around one small berry, pouring all of their hopes and desires into it. She desperately wished she could have seen it. *The trees full of birds of all shapes and sizes, the ground full of . . .* something tugged on her sleeve, snapping her out of it.

"What is *that*?" Diego pointed ahead on the shore.

Several black-winged creatures were swirling around in the sky, leaving a trail of smoke behind them as if they were on fire. They were all different shapes and sizes, but there was one that Olivia couldn't keep her eyes off. It was absolutely massive. She felt a sudden hot panic rise in her throat, knowing instinctively what they were.

"Brumas!" Tique darted underwater.

"Eek!" Ruda screeched, flattening her chest against the bottom of the boat. "Newen, what do we do?"

"Swim away!" said Tique, peeking out from the back of the dalca. "They can't get us underwater! Come on, get out! Quick, quick!"

Diego shot Olivia a nervous glance.

"That's not really an option for us," she said.

"Oh no no no!" said Tique frantically. "Can't outrun them by land. I'm sorry, I am, but I must go! Good luck, good luck!" With that, the otter vanished underwater.

"Good for nothing!" Ruda hissed at the otter's water ripples. "Slimy snake of a mammal!"

"Ruda, quiet!" Newen circled in the water. "We will go to shore. Everyone, climb on. Quickly."

Ruda leaped out of the dalca, landing directly on Newen's head.

With her one front paw, she held her fluffy tail away from the water. With this, she motioned for the others to follow. Diego splashed into the water, grabbing hold of Newen's back.

Olivia glanced back toward the swirling mass of smoke. The Brumas seemed to be flying in faster, smaller circles now, tightening in on something curled up on the ground. Something brown with just a little stripe of green.

"Max!" shouted Olivia, before diving headfirst into the river. The water was so crystal clear that the sunlight pierced through to the very bottom, illuminating every rock and fish and plant. Kicking her skinny legs behind her, Olivia propelled herself past an oblivious school of tiny silver fish. Eventually she reached the point where the ground climbed upward. Toward the shore. Toward Max. Toward whatever those things were.

Coming up for air, Olivia found herself a few yards away. She sprinted out of the water, her wet clothes weighing her down.

"Get out of here!" She shouted, arms waving about wildly. "Leave him alone!"

A gray mist poured down in front of her. Without hesitating, Olivia plunged into it.

She searched desperately for Max, but it was too foggy to see anything. He had to be here somewhere. She had definitely seen him. Hadn't she? Blindly reaching one hand into the mist, she inched forward. A strange heaviness washed over her, sinking deep into her bones. After two more steps, her hand fell limp, and she stood frozen in place, unable to move. Even her eyelids succumbed to the heaviness, slipping downwards, blanketing the last ounce of sunlight. Her ears were the last to go. She could barely hear the Brumas circling around her, with their spine-tingling humming.

She could hear something else, like a small whimper. Olivia forced her eyes to open, forced her foot off the ground. One. Then the other. Her legs felt weak, like she had just run ten laps at soccer practice. Every step forward took all the strength she had. In the distance, a small round shape began to take form. Olivia collapsed, crawling closer. When she reached the curled-up silhouette, everything blurred and went quiet.

Olivia looked around. It was dark. Where was she? It felt like she had just woken from a heavy slumber. She couldn't remember what she had been looking for, or anything at all, as if her memory had been wiped clean. She took a step forward and tripped on something on the ground. Feeling around in the darkness, she found a cord, which she followed with her fingers until she found its switch. She turned it on. In the dim lamplight, a wall appeared in front of her. It was painted sky blue with a big yellow sun in the corner. White clouds were sponged on here and there.

Olivia knew these walls. It was coming back to her, slowly. Ma had painted the cloud shaped like a pig, over there. Dad had done this one. He had tried to make a dragon, but they had all laughed at how fat it was. It was mutually decided that it wasn't a dragon, but a flying cow. Olivia smiled and turned to the cloud to her right, shaped like a dog. This masterpiece had been hers, of course. As she ran her fingers over the bumpy paint, she felt a vague sense of urgency.

The floor creaked behind her. She jumped and turned to look.

A brown and black striped dog came running up to her. Her heart leapt as if it were happy to see him, although she couldn't explain why. He seemed familiar somehow, but she didn't recognize him.

"Hi there, little doggy!" Olivia bent over to squish his cheeks. "You're so cute, I could just—"

"Listen to me," said a voice she did not recognize, a voice coming straight from the dog's mouth.

"What, how are—"

"This place," the dog continued. His voice was serious and tense. "It's all wrong. We have to get out of here."

"What do you mean?" asked Olivia, looking around. "Everything seems fine to me."

"Olivia, wake UP!" The dog jumped onto her chest.

Olivia smelled a whiff of chamomile puppy shampoo, and everything flashed back to her. The Brumas, Newen, Ruda, Diego, the strange forest, the huge alerce tree, and . . .

"Max!" Olivia dropped to her knees and threw her arms around him, squeezing tightly. "I've been so worried about you. I—"

The door handle rattled behind them. Max's hair spiked on the back of his neck. Whatever was on the other side of the door, he saw it as a threat.

"Olivia!"

She knew that voice, but it sounded different. Distorted, somehow.

"Olivia . . . help me."

Olivia inched forward, but Max shot out in front of her, blocking her path.

"Don't trust it. It's wrong, all wrong," Max repeated.

"Olivia, let me in."

The door handle shook violently. Olivia's eyes widened. She didn't know what it was, but she could feel it too. It was wrong. *All wrong.* Turning off the lamp, she crawled under the bed. Max followed, and she held onto him tightly. The door creaked open, the light from the hall spilling in. From under the bed, Olivia could see the dark silhouette of long legs standing in the doorway. She pressed her face into Max's fur and closed her eyes.

Creak . . .

Creeeak . . .

Creeeeeeak . . .

She could feel it standing right in front of them now, so close she could taste its rotten stench seeping under the bed. Holding her breath, she pressed her face even deeper into Max's fur.

He howled his worst high-pitched I'm-in-pain howl. Before Olivia could open her eyes, Max was swept out from under the bed. He continued to yelp in pain, his claws scratching a long line through the hardwood floor. Olivia propelled herself out from under the bed. A quick succession of *thud-thud-thuds* told her that

Max was being dragged down the stairs. Heart pounding high up in her throat, Olivia raced after him, leaping downward three steps at a time.

As she reached the first floor, two yellow eyes flashed before her. She recognized them, perhaps from a dream. In another flash, a clash of wings. *What's happening?* No time to think. She turned the corner into the living room.

That's when she saw it. The moonlight poured in from the window behind it, illuminating the abnormally tall and slim figure shrouded in a black hood. From within its sunken shadow of a face glowed two blank white eyes, burning into her. It stretched out one long black arm, wrapping its razor-sharp claws around Max's neck.

Olivia knew what this horrible thing was, for it was not the first time she had felt its presence. Yet somehow, at this moment, she felt no fear. What she felt was anger. No. Frustration. Fury. *Rage.*

Planting her feet firmly on the ground, Olivia glared directly at it. "Not this one. Let him go."

The creature lowered its jaw and emitted one long blood-curdling hiss. It tightened its grip, and Max yelped, struggling to get free.

Heart racing, Olivia demanded once more, "Let. Him. GO!"

The voice that spilled out of her was an unrecognizable, feral shriek. It echoed throughout the house, crashing into the walls. The ground shook, harder and harder, shattering the windows into a million pieces. The long black claws loosened their grip. The creature lowered its jaw once more, but before it could make a sound, it dissolved into dust.

As Olivia took a step forward, everything turned to black.

11.
RIVER COUNCIL

CONSCIOUSNESS SLOWLY LEAKED back in. Several voices murmured back and forth. Olivia did not recognize them, and she could not yet muster enough strength to open her eyes to see who the voices belonged to. She could barely make out what they were saying.

"Don't touch it! You saw what it did," shrieked an angry high-pitched voice.

"She's not an *it*, she's a human." *That sounds like Ruda,* thought Olivia as her head cleared.

"A WHAT?" said the same voice from before, followed by a chorus of questions from all around.

"A human?"

"How did it get in?"

"What do we do with it?"

"What will it do to US?"

"Hey, I'm a human too!" Diego's voice broke through the others. Another angry chorus of questions and accusations rang out until Newen's voice boomed over them. "THESE humans are with us," he said. "They will not harm you."

"But look what this one did to the forest!" said the first angry voice.

What did I do? The last thing she remembered was the horrible creature holding Max's life in its claws, a loud shriek, and everything shaking before turning black.

Slowly, Olivia cracked open an eye. The sky above was spinning like a kaleidoscope. Rubbing the last ounce of dizziness from her eyes, she turned to find Diego helping her up.

"Are you okay?" he asked, gently squeezing her shoulder.

"I . . . I don't know. What happened?"

"Oh man, it was CRAZY!" Eyes wide, Diego began wildly miming the recent events. "You ran straight into this big gray tornado. It was like WHOOOOOSSSHHHH, and we couldn't see you at all, but we followed you, and I took out my slingshot and was like BANG and shot one of those Brumas down. And this owl came and was fighting them too. And suddenly it was like BOOOOOM! Everything shook and fell everywhere. And, well, that's pretty much it, I think. You don't remember anything?"

"I remember—" Olivia noticed who was curled up on the ground beside her. "Max!"

Throwing herself over him, she wept, tears soaking into his warm fur. She didn't care who was watching. She was sure she looked like a pathetic, blubbering cry-baby, but she didn't care. With each tear, she felt lighter, each drop washing away an ounce of pain. After what felt like weeks wandering around this insane forest, finally, finally, she had found him. *I found Max! I found Max!* She couldn't stop repeating it. *We can go home now. Finally!*

Olivia wiped her jacket sleeve across her cheeks and nose. She ran her fingers across the length of Max's back, but he didn't move. Olivia panicked, all of her fear and anger and desperation flooding in. *He can't be dead, he just can't!* She shook him gently, but he didn't wake up. Putting her head on his belly, she felt it slowly sink and expand. *He's alive!* With a huge sigh of relief, she cupped his head in her hands and gently placed it in her lap, caressing his cheek.

"It may take some time for him to recover," squeaked a small voice.

Olivia's head spun around.

"Over here," said the voice.

Olivia looked down and, to her surprise, saw a small rodent staring up at her. She looked similar to Mandy's pet hamster Missy, with the same big beady eyes and brown and white fur. But unlike Missy the hamster, this rodent's nose was much pointier, and she had a very long tail where Missy had none.

"A little mouse!" said Olivia.

This comment caused another stir with the animals. Olivia heard, "How dare she!" and "Show some respect!" *This little rodent must be very important.*

"Oh, I'm sorry, I—"

"Quiet!" The tiny rodent hopped onto a rock, and the crowd fell silent. "It's quite alright. Perhaps it would help if we introduced ourselves. We are the River Council. It is our job to keep peace in the forest."

The rodent went around the clearing, introducing each and every animal present. They were all standing somewhat far away, as if scared to get too close. To Olivia's left, several birds were perched on a log—little gray birds, large blue birds, fat orange birds, and one bird that she swore had seven different colors. To her right, beneath the huge nalca leaves, sat a miniature spotted leopard with a sour face, two tiny deer, and a handful of different-colored frogs. Even Tique the otter was there, covered in mud. He didn't look at all guilty for having abandoned them.

"Rayen, Ayelen, Boldo, Tique, Tucu, Newen and Ruda, who I believe you know." Newen nodded solemnly as Ruda fluffed her tail with pride. "And my name is Maqui. I am not a mouse as you have said. I am a *monito del monte.*"

"Oh, cool!" said Diego, crouching down to the

ground. "I've heard of you. You're like a tiny kangaroo. Can I see your pouch?"

For the last time the animals erupted in indignation. Ruda buried her face in her tail.

"Oh, geeze, sorry!" said Diego. "It's just . . . you're so cool! I've read all about you, but never seen one. And regular mice don't have pouches so I thought . . . Oh!"

Diego slapped his hand over his mouth, realizing too late that he had used the forbidden *M* word again. Olivia held her breath, but to her surprise, the *monito del monte* did not look angry at all. In fact, she cracked a smile, then squeaked out a high-pitched laugh, her pink paws holding on to her belly as she rocked back and forth.

"Oh my! You truly are a curious little creature. This must all be new for you. Well, you see, you're new for us as well. We've never had humans in our forest before, and some of us are somewhat concerned."

"More than concerned!" shouted the first angry voice Olivia had heard, which she now saw belonged to Boldo, the spotted kodkod cat. "Someone please tell these humans to leave before they destroy us all!"

"Dear Olivia and Diego," said Ruda, standing tall on her hind legs. "Boldo says that it is his honor to welcome you to our forest."

"That is NOT what I said!" screeched Boldo. "Tell them that they—"

"Boldo says that if you need anything during your stay," continued Ruda, "please let him know, and he will be happy to—"

"Is this a joke to you, Ruda?" spat Boldo. "We'll see if you're still laughing when they start killing us all, one by one. Everyone, listen to me. The humans must be sent back immediately. Or better yet, send them to the volcano for Kutral to deal with!"

"Bite your tongue, you filthy feline!" yelled Ruda.

"Stay out of this, vixen!" hissed Boldo.

Ruda arched her back and puffed up her hackles to make herself appear larger. Boldo followed suit, both animals in a stand-off position.

"Ruda, Boldo, that's ENOUGH!" thundered Maqui, with her little brows furrowed and her little paws on her hips. "You've spoken your part, Boldo, now it's time to sit and listen. Quietly."

Boldo stuck his nose in the air.

The little *monito del monte* looked at Olivia once more, inspecting how she ran her fingers through Max's fur. She hadn't let go of him once.

"Does this animal mean something to you?"

"Yes. We're family," Olivia frowned. "Why is that so hard for everyone to understand?"

Maqui's large beady eyes swelled. "I never thought I'd hear a human say that, but I'm glad I did."

"Please!" said Olivia, looking down. "What's wrong with him?"

"He appears to have been injured in the river. When the Brumas came, he could not run away. I'm afraid he was under their spell for quite some time. Even to a very strong, large animal, they can be harmful."

"But how?" asked Olivia.

"They use the Energy to get into your head and make you see things. They play with your worst fears. The longer you're under their spell, the worse it becomes."

Olivia swallowed hard. "But he'll recover, right? He'll be okay?"

There was a short pause just long enough to be unbearable.

"With time." Maqui hopped closer. "It's clear that you two have an incredibly strong bond. We've never seen any creature do what you did."

"What do you mean? What did I do?"

"Destroy half the forest, that's what!" spat Boldo in disgust.

"What do you—" Olivia stopped herself. She had been so distracted with Max and the River Council that she hadn't taken a moment to take in her surroundings. Forming a semicircle around her, a large number of trees and other plants lay fallen. Black feathers that appeared to be burnt were scattered about here and there. On top of an abnormally large pile of feathers lay a round black heap of something. As Olivia studied it further, she realized it was a bird laying belly up. But it was a truly massive bird, at least ten times as large as Tucu the owl. She had never seen a bird so big. It was like looking at a dragon who had been shot down, his long talons pointing up, his wings splayed out on either side. *Is this a Bruma?* Olivia swallowed hard. Even if it had been attacking her, she hated seeing it laying lifeless. She then noticed something even more curious. The fallen trees were all pointing outward, away from her, as if some strong impact had taken place where she was sitting.

"I didn't . . . I did this?" Olivia looked at Newen. He nodded.

"It appears as though the Energy runs strong in Olivia," said Newen. "She is learning to control her emotions. This will not happen again."

"Remind me, Newen," said Boldo. "Who else had such powerful emotions? Or have you forgotten already?"

There was a collective gasp. Newen dug his claws into the dirt, but after a few seconds he released his grip and began pacing back and forth like a lion at the zoo.

Tucu broke his silence. "Let us not judge Olivia too soon. I sense grief and anger inside of her, yes, but I also sense kindness and love. Her journey is only beginning, and it's not for us to say which path she'll choose."

The owl twisted his head until it pointed in Olivia's direction. His large yellow eyes pierced straight into her own. It made her uneasy. She studied him for any visible sign of hope or fear or empathy, anything at all, but there was nothing there. He stared, expressionless, silent. Unable to take it anymore, Olivia tore her eyes away, breaking their connection.

The *monito del monte* scampered back and forth, frowning. She hopped over to Olivia's shoe, used her long fingers to grip the fabric of her jeans, and then climbed up her legs. Once she got to Olivia's knee, she stopped and tilted her head, curious.

"I wonder. No one has ever been able to . . . but maybe she could . . . well, now that's a thought, but it's risky." Maqui seemed to be talking more to herself than to Olivia.

"Maybe I could *what*?" Olivia asked.

Maqui looked up with her large round eyes.

"Maybe you could save us."

12.
LAST CANELO BERRY

MAYBE OLIVIA COULD save them? But save them from what?

"What do you mean?" Olivia frowned. "And why would I, of all people, or uh, animals, be able to—"

"You see, our forest—" Maqui began, but Boldo cut her off, as angry as ever.

"DON'T tell her anything!"

"Boldo, please," said Maqui. "She may be able to help."

"We don't know that for sure!" screeched the little cat.

"Hmmm, you may be right. Maybe we should see if . . . " Maqui turned back to Olivia, twitching her fluffy eyebrows. "Can you control it?"

"Control what?" Olivia still wasn't following any of what was going on.

"Control what?" Boldo said, mocking Olivia. "Honestly, Maqui, this human is as dumb as a slug."

One of the spotted snails stuck its tongue out.

Maqui shushed Boldo, turning back to Olivia. "The *Energy*, of course! Have you tried to make things happen, not when you're angry? For example, can you make things grow?"

What kind of a question is that? Do they think I have superpowers?

Olivia fidgeted with Max's toes, thinking back to the strange occurrences over the last couple days.

"I, uh . . . I don't know," said Olivia. "Everything so far has sort of happened without me even thinking about it. So for me to try to make something grow, I wouldn't know where to start."

Maqui hopped off of Olivia's knee and scratched at the dirt in front of her. "This soil is filled with seeds that are waiting to receive enough sunlight to be able to shoot out of the ground. If you can give them sun, you can make them grow."

Olivia frowned. This little rodent couldn't possibly think that she had control over the sunlight.

"Come on, Olivia! You can do it!" shouted Diego enthusiastically. Newen and Ruda nodded.

Olivia shook her head but decided to give it a try. She put her hand out over the ground and closed her eyes. Not sure what else to do, she imagined that she could make beams of light shoot out of the center of her palm like the White Wolf. She focused on this thought for a minute, until her mind wandered. *Are they ever going to make a sequel to The White Wolf? Will I have to watch it in Spanish? And—*

Olivia snapped herself out of it, peeking open an eye. Nothing had happened. No light, no magic, nothing.

"Sorry," she shrugged. She hadn't really expected anything to happen, but she couldn't help feeling disappointed. There was no way she would let them know that, though.

Maqui sighed and hopped off of Olivia's knee. Newen walked closer and lowered his head to her eye level. "Olivia, tell me about Max. Tell me why you consider him family."

Olivia dropped her gaze to the sleeping dog in her lap. She was a bit confused as to why he was asking her to do this, but she obeyed. "Well, I don't have any siblings, so I've always thought of Max as my brother. He goes everywhere I go—the beach, bike rides, Scout meetings. He even walks me to the bus every morning. He's not allowed to go to school with me, which I don't think is fair because Annelise Davison brings her floofy little toy poodle to school and says that she's an emotional support dog, and everyone knows that's a total load of—"

Ruda cleared her throat and raised her eyebrows. Olivia understood the message; *stay on track.*

"Oh, sorry. Um . . . what else? Well, Max sleeps in my bed with me every night. So, if I have a nightmare, I reach over, and he's there. He makes me feel safe. Oh, and he sleeps in funny positions, like on his back with his paws in the air, and sometimes he runs in his sleep, so it looks like he's trying to fly upside down. And he snores like an old man!"

Olivia giggled. Wiping away a tear of joy, she continued. "He makes me happy. And things haven't been so happy lately, ever since—" She trailed off.

"That's okay. You don't have to talk about that," said Newen. "Why don't you tell me how he makes you feel better when you're sad?"

"Little things. Like I scratch him behind his ear, and he wags his tail and puts his head on my lap. And I talk to him sometimes at night about how I feel. I know it sounds silly, but I feel like he understands me. He doesn't say anything back, of course. It's not like here, where animals can talk. But still, he looks at me with his soft eyes, or he rubs his head on my chest, and that's enough to make me feel not so alone."

Olivia looked up. All of the animals were silently staring at the same spot in the center of the clearing where a bright white beam of sunlight was shining on a dozen tiny green pods poking up from the ground. Olivia looked at the sky, realizing what must have happened. As she had been talking, the clouds above her had drifted apart, creating an opening wide enough for the sunlight to escape. By the time she glanced at the ground, leaves had already begun sprouting out from the tiny stems.

Olivia was speechless.

"You have an incredible gift," said Maqui, looking hopeful once more.

"Hey, how come I can't do that?" Diego pouted, not attempting to hide his jealousy one bit.

"The Energy runs through you and every one of us, but not everyone can use it the way Olivia can," said Maqui. "Some think that those who have experienced a tragedy can feel it more strongly. We aren't certain, but what we do know is that the Energy is fading. Trees are dying and our water sources are drying up. The doorway into this forest is beginning to break open. We don't know how much longer it will last. But you, Olivia, maybe, just maybe, you can help us."

Olivia frowned. "I don't think—"

"It isn't about what you think, it's about what you feel." Maqui hopped back onto Olivia's knee and climbed up her jacket zipper. She was extremely quick and nimble, reaching Olivia's chest in two seconds. Once there, she placed her tiny paw over Olivia's heart.

"The Heart!" shouted Tique the otter.

"She can heal the Heart!" croaked a frog on a log.

"The Heart . . . The Heart . . . The Heart . . ." echoed throughout the crowded space, in the water, on the rocks, in the trees, until it became a chant. Maqui held up her paw once more, demanding silence.

"Near the volcano, there is a pond of water where all the roots in this entire forest intertwine," began Maqui. "They carry with them the Energy from every single creature and plant, merging it all together, and then pumping it back out once more. This living, beating heart has maintained the flow of the Energy here, but it is only as strong as all the living things feeding into it. Every day a tree dies, the Heart loses strength. It means our forest is dying. We need your help to heal it."

"I can't grow an entire forest," said Olivia, shaking her head. "I don't think I'm as strong as you think I am."

Maqui shook her head. "No. You *alone* cannot heal the forest. But with this, perhaps you can."

The little *monito del monte* reached down into her pouch and pulled out a large blueish-black berry with white flecks. It was irradiating a bright light.

Olivia heard Diego whisper, "A pouch, I knew it!"

"This berry is from the last sacred canelo tree that existed in this forest. We have used many of them in the past, but this is the only one we have left. All of us here have bestowed some of our Energy, and with it our hopes and desires, into this one last berry. We are hoping that this will be enough to give new life to the forest."

"So, what do you want me to do with it?"

"It must be planted in the Heart of the Forest, where it will have the greatest impact."

"But why do you need me to take it? Wouldn't it be easier for Tucu or one of the other birds to fly it there?"

"We have tried," said Tucu, still perched in a branch above them. "We can't get close enough. The Heart is guarded by Brumas."

"Why would they want the forest to die?" asked Diego. "They're animals too, aren't they?"

"Yes, the Brumas are animals like us, or at least they were at some point. They were all scavengers, like this condor here." Maqui pointed her little snout toward the huge fallen bird. "They never liked it here. Too much peace, and not enough death for them to feed on. So long ago they made a deal with Kutral. He gave them power, and in return they go where he cannot, and act on his behalf."

"So he wants the forest to die?" asked Diego.

Maqui shook her little head. "Not die completely, no. We think he's waiting for the Energy to deteriorate until it becomes so weak that the barrier keeping him trapped at the volcano will evaporate. By that point, the doorway between forests will have broken open, and he'll be free to leave, and free to go to the other side."

"And finish what he started," Newen sighed.

Maqui wiggled her whiskers. "You, Olivia, are the only one we've seen who is strong enough to escape the Bruma's spell. It did come at a cost, but now you've proven that you could be trained to use the Energy for good. That is why we need you to take it. Will you help us?"

Olivia wished she weren't here, surrounded by an entire community of animals counting on her. As much as she wanted to be a hero in her everyday life, she didn't feel like being one now that she was needed.

"I . . . I don't—" Before Olivia could finish her sentence, she felt movement in her lap. Max was beginning to stir. His nose and paws were twitching, and his eyes slowly blinked.

"Max!" Olivia cried. She scooped up his head ever so gently. "Maxy, can you hear me?"

"Olivia?" whispered her dog in the same voice from her vision.

A heavy tear splashed down Olivia's cheek. "I'm here."

"What happened?" Max asked.

"You got lost in the forest, but I found you. You're gonna be okay. We're going home now."

"But they need you to . . . help with something?"

Olivia looked at all the animals staring at her expectantly.

"Please, can we have a moment alone?" she asked, wiping away a tear.

Maqui nodded, and all the others scurried off into the forest one by one, with Diego the last to go. Before vanishing into the thicket, he grinned at her, giving a big thumbs up.

Olivia looked at Max, still caressing the soft fur around his neck.

"Don't worry about what you heard, okay? I'm going to take you home and—"

"But I'm fine, I can go with you." Max tried to lift himself off the ground, but he collapsed after one step, yelping and licking his left front paw.

"Max, please," said Olivia, gently rubbing his back. "You're hurt. You need to rest."

"You should go," said Max. "You should help them."

"I'm not going to leave you here."

"Fine, then I'll go home, and you can go on without me."

Olivia shook her head. "Why do you want me to do this so badly?"

"Because it's what Dad would have wanted you to do, right?"

Olivia froze. "How do you know that? Could you understand him?"

"Not his words, no, but I saw how every time he talked to you, you felt stronger afterwards. Braver."

Olivia grinned. "Yeah, he would always tell me to be the hero."

"So what's stopping you?"

Olivia sighed. "I can't . . . I can't save everyone! And I'm not losing anyone else in my family. So I'm sorry for them, but they're on their own."

"You wouldn't really turn your back on them when they need help, would you?"

Olivia hesitated. "If they're asking me to choose between them and you, I choose you. You're the only real friend I've got left. I'm not leaving you. And that's it."

Max blinked at her, wrinkling his nose. "You know, when I was in . . . whatever that place was . . . you know what I saw?"

Olivia shook her head.

"I was back in those woods where you first found me, waiting. You rode by on your bike, and I knew you were there to rescue me, but you didn't. You looked at me like I was nothing, and you just kept pedaling. So I waited another day, but you didn't stop. Not the next day either. You never stopped for me. I even started to run after you, but you pedaled faster. Now I know, and I felt even then, that it wasn't *my* Olivia."

"No, I would never leave you there! I came all this way to find you!"

Max licked the palm of her hand. "I know. But the thing is, well, even if my head is foggy and my paws aren't right, my nose still seems to be working fine." He sniffed at the fabric of her jeans. "And

I know for certain there were a couple mammals and a human boy here, and I know you must've been with them for a while because their smell is all over you. So when you say I'm the only friend you've got left, well, it seems like you've made friends and you can't even see it. Now they're asking you for help, and you're going to turn your back on them? That's not *my* Olivia. That's not the Olivia who stopped her bike, fed me peanut butter sandwiches, took me home, and made me a part of her family. Where did that Olivia go?"

"I'm still here, but things have changed."

"Why? Because Dad died? You can't use his death as an excuse to be afraid to try something. And that's all these animals are asking you to do. Try."

Olivia knew Max was right, but her fear wasn't easy to shake off.

"What if I try to help them and I fail? It will be my fault."

"Like it was with Dad? That wasn't your fault."

Olivia froze. "So, you did understand me? All those nights, when I told you those things?"

"I could feel how you felt. Dogs are special that way, you know." Max rubbed his head against Olivia's knee.

Olivia smiled. "I knew it. You always understood me. Not like everyone else."

"You know I'll always be here for you to talk to. Always, *always*. But it might surprise you how it feels to open up to others. They might understand more than you think."

"Maybe, I don't know," Olivia sighed. "Hey, when did you get so wise?"

Olivia scratched Max in his favorite spot under his chin. He smiled, his tail thumping against the ground. An incredible weight lifted from her chest, seeing him returning to his old self. She knew he was right about everything, but her stomach once again filled with anxious butterflies thinking about leaving him.

"Are you sure you'll be okay without me?"

"I'll be fine. And like I said, I know you'll always come back for me."

"Always, *always*," said Olivia, smiling.

13.

✦ONE WITH THE WIND

OLIVIA TUCKED A rolled up nalca leaf into Max's collar.

"Are you sure you're going to be okay?" she asked him.

"I'll be fine! Good as new, see?" Max jumped up and down on his back paws.

Olivia had been hoping for a little more time to spend with him before leaving, but she couldn't keep stalling. His injury had healed, and he was already back to his normal goofy-doggy self. It was amazing what a few magical copihue flowers and some snail slime could do. If only it were always that easy!

"So, you really don't want me to come with you?" Max asked, instantly turning on the puppy eyes to full effect.

"Yes, we've been over this! I'm not putting you in any more danger. Plus, you have the most important task of all. You remember what you have to do, right?" Olivia asked for the third time.

"Yes, I got it, I got it!" Max twirled around in a circle. "Make sure Ma checks my collar so she gets the message that you and Diego are okay and will be back soon. Don't worry!"

"Pinza will show him the way back," said Maqui, nodding to a bright green hummingbird whose wings beat so fast they blurred. "And Antu will fly above them, looking out for Brumas so they don't get into any trouble." A smaller, rounder owl bobbed its head just like Tucu always did.

Olivia glanced at Diego, currently playing peekaboo with the baby Pudu deer. "Diego, are you sure you don't want to go back too?"

"Not this again! I'm coming with you and that's final," he replied, not looking up from his game. Olivia thought she saw a small eye roll before he hid his face in his hands once more.

So it was decided, then. There wasn't anything left to do but say goodbye to Max. Olivia pressed her forehead against his and then wrapped her arms around him. She ran her fingers through every inch of his fur, from the baby-soft hairs lining his ears, to the wiry scruff of his neck, and down to scratch the wisp of fur covering his warm belly.

She and Max were supposed to be inseparable, yet this was the second time since arriving here that they would part ways. And this time it was her choice. Before Olivia could change her mind, she straightened up and took two steps backward.

"Take care of Ma until I get back, okay?"

"You don't worry about us," Max said. "They need you here. I know you can do it. You've got this!"

"Thanks, Max," said Olivia, her voice cracking. "You're such a good boy. The best."

Max thwapped his tail against the ground, happy to have received the highest compliment a dog could ever hope for.

Olivia gave him one last kiss in the dip of his temple. Unable to say goodbye, she said instead, "Well, go on, then!" and gave him a small pat on the rump.

Max turned and sprinted off into the forest, an owl and hummingbird right behind him.

Just as Olivia's heart was about to split, something soft rubbed against her knees. Ruda's speckled face blinked up at her. Olivia wrapped her arms around the fox, happily accepting the comfort she offered.

"Well, then!" Maqui clapped her pink paws together. "No time to waste. Off you go, all of you! You know your roles."

"Roles?" Olivia asked as each of the animals scurried in different directions. "What—" She searched for someone to explain, only to find Newen wading into the river and Ruda disappearing into the forest. Diego dragged one of the fallen tree trunks toward the shore and began tearing off its branches. Maqui supervised, sitting tall on her perch on Diego's shoulder.

A splash to Olivia's right announced Newen's return to shore, pushing the abandoned dalca in front of him. Grabbing hold, Diego helped pull it in. He took a moment to inspect it as Maqui whispered in his ear. He nodded and knocked on its side in two strategic locations.

"Here and here," he said, as two red-headed woodpeckers landed on the boat's edge and began drilling holes into the two spots that Diego had indicated.

Ruda returned from the forest pulling a long bamboo-like stick behind her. She deposited it by Diego's feet before prancing off for another.

"Will someone please explain what's going on?" Olivia asked.

Diego looked up briefly, his eyes shining bright. "We're going to *sail* there!"

Sensing that was as much information as she was going to get out of anyone, Olivia decided she might as well make herself useful. She turned to find more sticks to add to Ruda's pile, but before she took a step, Tucu called to her.

"You have other work to do," said the owl.

"Sure, you need me to fetch something else?" Olivia responded, pleased that someone was actually communicating with her.

The owl bobbed his head before leaping into the air. He circled overhead twice before diving to land across the river. Extending his right wing, he plucked a single feather from his flank, depositing it amongst the pebbles and twigs littering the rivershore. Seemingly satisfied, he flew back to join Olivia.

"I need you to bring me my feather."

Olivia wrinkled her nose, not at all understanding the purpose of this task. Annoyed at the prospect of getting wet again, she begrudgingly untied one of her boots. Tucu stopped her.

"Remain where you are," said Tucu, "and bring the feather here."

"What? But how am I supposed to—" It took a few seconds before the realization hit her. If she didn't have to swim across to retrieve the feather, then Tucu expected her to use the Energy to retrieve it. Now it made sense. *This must be like the classic training scene in a superhero movie, like when Suzie Skink taught White Wolf how to control her powers.* And now it was Olivia's turn, with Tucu acting as the proverbial sensei.

To get the feather across the river, she'd need wind. She remembered the technique Newen had taught her to build the fire. Step one, close her eyes. Step two, breathe slowly. She inhaled for five Mississippi-seconds, feeling her belly expand until it pressed against the waistline of her pants. She held it in for another second before letting it go. The next step had been to imagine a warm fire building inside her. Maybe this time it would help to focus on the feeling of the wind instead. *Inhale.* The wind blowing through her hair. *Exhale.* The cold against her skin. Tiny hairs tickling her arm. *Inhale.* The crisp smell of nature. The soft rustling of a hundred leaves.

Exhaling once more, Olivia opened her eyes. The feather struggled to get off the ground, nudged ever so slightly by a soft breeze. She would need more than that to blow it across the river. She closed her eyes and repeated the breathing exercise for several more cycles, imagining a stronger wind each time. Finally, the feather broke free from the earth, dancing around in small circles.

"Good," said Tucu. "Keep it coming."

Olivia continued to fill her chest with as much air as she could, holding it in, then letting it spill out of her until the last drop. All the while she focused on the wind.

Olivia peeked open her eyes, glimpsing the feather halfway across the river. Then, in a blink, she saw an animal struggling to keep his head above the water. *It looks like—*

Olivia jumped to her feet, but as soon as she did, he was gone.
"Tucu, did you see—"

"No need to panic. It was only an illusion," replied the owl. "I showed you a few seconds of something you feared. That's all it took to distract you from your task. Now the feather has fallen into the water."

"What? Why would you show me that on purpose? That is *so* mean!" Olivia's cheeks burned with anger.

"You must learn control. The Brumas will attempt to manipulate your emotions by showing you visions. They want to anger you, scare you, trick you into believing falsehoods."

"I've seen what they do," said Olivia, crossing her arms. "I can handle them."

"Yes, we've seen that. And how many of our trees do you think you'll destroy next time?"

"What? That's not fair," said Olivia. "That was different. That *thing* had Max."

"And that made you angry, didn't it?"

"Of course! So what? I saved him, didn't I?"

"But at what cost?"

Olivia silently stared into the owl's unwavering golden gaze. She knew he was right. He was always right, a trait that annoyed her more than usual right now. She sighed in defeat.

"I get it. My anger is destructive. So, are you going to teach me to control it or not?"

"I can help guide you, but only you can discover what works best for you. Some meditate, others have a mantra."

"A mantra?"

"Yes. A mantra is a positive thought or word that you repeat to yourself. It should be something that makes you feel happy and peaceful. Why don't you give it a try? Close your eyes, breathe deeply, and try to think of your mantra."

Olivia closed her eyes once more. *Family*, she thought. *Scouts . . . Soccer. . . Camping?* None of them seemed to calm her. What had once been some of the happiest words in the world were now heavy with mixed emotions. What made her happy *now*? It had been a long time since she felt pure joy.

A scene appeared in Olivia's head. She was sitting on the couch, wrapped in her favorite fluffy blanket that smelled like sand and salt. Max was balled up at her feet as always. They were watching the *White Wolf* for the twentieth time, with Olivia repeating the lines she had memorized long ago. Ma handed her a steaming hot mug of her famous *chocolate submarine*. A thousand times better than regular hot cocoa, it was made by dropping a bar of chocolate into a pool of boiling milk and stirring it up in a swirl. Chocolate submarines were so good that they could always lift her spirits.

Olivia smiled. She was sure that a mantra was supposed to be something more profound, but this seemed to fit her. "Okay, I've got it."

Tucu deposited a new, dry feather on the opposite side of the river, and for the third time Olivia closed her eyes.

She concentrated as hard as she could on her new mantra until she could see the mug and feel its warmth between her hands. She could smell the chocolate melting into the boiling milk. She held in this scent for a moment, watching the beige and brown rings dance around her spoon. She blew on the top of the mug, cooling it. When she went to take a sip, the image of Max struggling against the river's strong current flashed in her mind, breaking her concentration. She shook her head, forcing herself to focus on her mantra once more.

Pulling the fluffy blanket higher, she sank down into the couch, watching as the White Wolf destroyed the bad guys. Before she could finish her drink, Ma was back to offer a refill. This time, she added double chocolate. As every negative image popped into her head, Olivia rejected it, replacing it with her *chocolate submarine.*

A sense of calm washed over her. The tension she didn't realize she was holding in her muscles disappeared, as well as any worries for the future. She was only here, in this moment, holding an imaginary mug of chocolate happiness.

Something tickled her cheek, waking her. Olivia opened her eyes. The feather had reached its destination.

Tucu made Olivia repeat the exercise for what felt like hours, making it a little bit harder each time. Eventually she had mastered it so well that she could even make her marbles spin around in the air. By the time Tucu allowed her to rejoin the others, construction on the dalca was nearly finished. She was shocked by what one boy and a group of animals had managed to build out of nothing but sticks and leaves.

At the front of the dalca, the tall tree trunk that Diego had cleaned bare stood as a mast. Attached to it was one large sail made from the bamboo-like sticks Ruda had fetched, with giant green nalca leaves woven throughout. Two smaller branches pierced through the holes that the woodpeckers had created in the sides of the dalca, stabilizing the tree-trunk mast.

"Diego, this is incredible," Olivia remarked while marveling at the sight of it. "How did you know how to build this?"

Diego laughed with a shrug. "I like to make things. Model planes and toy cars, my little sister's dollhouse, my slingshot . . . never made a sailboat before, though!"

"You leave as soon as the sun sets," said Maqui, still perched upon Diego's shoulder. "It will be safer to cross the lake at night."

Seeing how low the sun already was, Olivia estimated another hour of light before they would have to leave.

"You should rest now," said Tucu. "We will bring you food."

Diego and Olivia built another small fire to warm themselves as the animals scattered about in search of food. A small black snake slithered straight up to Newen, who lowered his head. Diego scooted backwards, looking like he'd just seen a ghost. When the snake finished whispering in Newen's ear, it turned, winked at the two humans and glided off. Diego exhaled as Newen rose, stretched his haunches, and then prowled into the thick woods.

Olivia frowned. "Does Newen . . . hunt?"

"Most pumas do," said Tucu. "That is their way. But Newen has come to an agreement with the River Council. He does not hunt us, and in return we inform him when an animal is very sick or has already died."

Diego's eyes grew wide. "So he, like . . . eats your dead friends?"

Tucu tilted his head. "Why, yes. But it is not as shocking as you seem to believe. When you die, your body will slowly decompose into the soil and turn to food for the worms. Or you could feed one very hungry puma. If you could choose beforehand, would you?"

"Oh," said Diego. "I guess I never thought of it that way. But yeah, if I knew that my body would help Newen survive, it would be an honor to be his dinner!"

Olivia's stomach churned. "Can we talk about something else please?" Trying to distract herself, she took two marbles out of her pocket and made them dance in midair.

Tucu narrowed his large round eyes. After a long pause, he said, "Your fear of death is dangerous. You will need to address it before it's too late."

"Add it to the list," Olivia mumbled, pulling two more marbles out and throwing them in the air to join the others.

The animals returned, producing the food they had gathered from the forest. Olivia and Diego each took their pick—large red berries for her and tiny black berries for him. Olivia's stomach instantly rejoiced as the first ripe berry burst into a sweet pulp between her teeth. She hadn't realized how hungry she was. Grabbing another greedy handful, she gulped it down.

Newen returned after some time, his paws and snout covered in blood.

Ruda's ears pricked forward. "Who?"

Newen cleaned the blood from the pads of his paws, speaking between licks. "Aliwen."

A high-pitched whine erupted from a baby Pudu deer. Her mother stood over her, head lowered. They huddled together in mourning.

"How did it happen?" asked the mother Pudu.

"A tree fell."

Ruda hung her head, ears flat back. "When will it end?"

"We must have faith that Olivia will succeed," said Maqui. "The forest will come back to life."

Olivia's chest tightened. All their hopes were placed on her shoulders. Now that they were about to leave, it was impossible for her to ignore the nagging question. She sighed. *Now or never.*

"If the trees are dying because of what's happening on our side of the forest, then how is this magic berry going to stop it from happening again in the future?"

Silence.

"We must have faith," said Maqui.

Faith. Olivia hated that word. Thinking of her father, she recalled being told, *"We have to have faith that he'll get better. Have faith, and everything will be okay."* But he didn't, and it wasn't.

"I'm sorry but—" Olivia froze. Hundreds of little faces stared at her. They were anxiously awaiting her next words, full of hope and fear and desperation. She had to be careful what she said next. "We can't just have *faith*. We have to do something. We have to stop the destruction on our end, otherwise trees will keep falling here."

"What do you propose we do then, human?" asked Boldo, scowling. "Hop on over and ask them politely to stop destroying our home? They can't even understand us."

"We'll be your voices!" said Olivia.

Boldo scoffed.

"She's right," said Diego. "Not all humans are bad. A lot of us love the forest. Don Pancho has been fighting to save it for years, but everyone says there's nothing left to save. Maybe they only need to see that you're still here."

"Never!" hissed Boldo. "We'd be skinned and cooked before you got two words out in our defense. I'd rather die here, where we're free, thank you very much."

"But—"

Maqui held up her paw. "Boldo is right. This is our home now. We can't go back. We must protect what we have here." She turned to Olivia, her eyes stern. "You must take the canelo berry to the Heart of the Forest. Have faith that it will work. Please."

Olivia nodded. Sensing that this discussion was over, she turned back to the dwindling pile of berries at her feet. They glowed orange by the light of the campfire, the sun having made its final descent below the horizon.

The truth was, Olivia wanted it to work as much as any of them. And she truly hoped that she could be the hero that they so desperately needed. But if they were asking her to simply have *faith* . . . the last time she had placed her faith in something, it had only let her down.

"It's time," Tucu announced.

14.

ALL THE STARS
IN THE SKY

WITH THEIR POCKETS stuffed with berries, Olivia and Diego made their final round of goodbyes.

"Take care of your mom, Rayen." Diego knelt, pressing his palm to the baby Pudu deer's cheek. She licked his wrist, making him giggle.

"We will help you get started," said Maqui. "After that, it will be up to you to keep the wind blowing. It will take all night to cross the lake, should all go well."

"I will fly ahead to look out for any Brumas," said Tucu.

"Once again," said Maqui. "Thank you, and good luck."

The last to board the dalca-turned-sailboat was Diego, giving it its final push into the water before hopping in. He took his place at the front, adjusting his all-natural sails before turning back and giving the signal to take off.

Tucu leapt into the night sky, his long wings silhouetted in the moonlight. The other animals of the River Council lined up along the shore. Some of them hung their heads and closed their eyes, as if in prayer, while others stared straight ahead. All remained silent.

It came quickly—a gust of wind crashing into the green sails, pulling them taut. The dalca dipped briefly before pulling up again. Olivia gripped the side of the boat, anticipating a bumpy journey, yet, in mere seconds, it stabilized itself. Before she knew it, they were gliding, effortlessly cutting through the dark water.

Olivia couldn't help but feel emotional. Good emotional. Excited. *Exhilarated*, even. Who would believe what they were doing, sailing along in a sailboat made of nothing but wood and leaves, pushed by a gust of wind created by a magical energy willed up by a group of talking animals? She could hardly even convince herself it was real.

She stared at the midnight hues of the night sky, the indigo blue stretching back into infinity. The lemony white moon climbed above the mountains' dark silhouette, floating into a sea of stars glowing a million times more intensely than Olivia had ever seen. The stars were not the only thing that glittered. With not a cloud in sight, the forest blinked with life. Little dots of light raced through the water like tiny fireflies. A pod of fish swam by the dalca and leapt out of the water, giving them a shimmering show.

Before rounding a bend in the river, Olivia caught one last glimpse at all the animals lining the shore. As the dalca continued cutting through the water's glassy surface, the glowing trees lining the shore dimmed until every last dot of light went out. All would have been pitch black if not for the full moon shining on the dark pointy stumps where fully grown trees had once stood.

"What happened here?" Ruda clawed the edge of the dalca, ears pointed forward. "Why have they all died?"

"It's like a tree graveyard," whispered Diego.

As they sailed around another bend in the river, the water level declined, causing the dalca to bump against the rocky bottom, skidding to a halt. Diego bent over the edge of the boat, inspecting the depth of the water with his hand. A short distance ahead of them, the river opened, spilling into the lake.

"Wait!" he announced. "I know where we are. This must be where they built the dam!"

"What is a dam?" asked Ruda, lowering her pointy snout to sniff the water's dark surface.

"It's like this big wall of stones," Diego spread his arms as wide as he could, "that stops the water from flowing."

"Why would you do something like that?"

"They use it to make energy or something."

"You can't make Energy." Ruda wrinkled her brow.

"No, not like that. I mean, well, I don't understand it. But don Pancho says that it's caused the lake water to decline a lot in the last ten years."

Ruda shook her head in disapproval. Newen leapt into the water. Without his considerable weight, the boat dislodged and wobbled. He waded to the back of the boat and pushed his head against the wood, nudging it forward. Diego grabbed the long skinny paddle and pushed down against the riverbed. Together they freed the boat from the river's bottleneck, releasing it into the lake.

Mission accomplished, Newen climbed back into the boat and promptly shook the water from his thick coat. With nowhere to hide, they all received a thorough soaking, but no one complained. They continued silently staring at the dark stumps silhouetted in the moonlight. No words were needed to express the feelings they shared.

"It's a straight path from here," said Newen, breaking the silence. "You should all try to sleep. I'll take the first shift."

Diego abandoned his post manning the sail, still pulled taut from the force of the wind, and scooted over to join the others. Ruda hopped onto his chest and curled into a ball. He cradled her furry back, sinking into Olivia's side and using her shoulder as a pillow. As Olivia listened to the lapping water and the soft breathing of Ruda and Diego, she felt more at peace than she had in some time. She hung her arm over the side of the boat, dipping the tip of her fingers into the icy water. Olivia watched the whites and yellows of the sky's starry reflection swirl into the blues and blacks of the water's dark surface until everything blurred together.

"If you feel a tug, start reeling this lever back in," said Dad, sitting next to Olivia. She knew this was a dream, but it felt real. She vividly remembered the day when she and her father sat in old metal beach chairs on a long wooden dock, both with fishing rods in hand. Behind them, Max snoozed with his belly in the air.

"What if it's too big for me? What if it pulls me in?" Olivia asked.

"I guess I'd have to find a new daughter then." Dad shrugged and waved toward the ocean. "Bye, Livy! Have fun with the fish!"

Olivia rolled her eyes playfully, all too used to his wacky sense of humor. "No, really!"

"Well, if you catch a big one, then I'll help you. But if you catch a whale, we'll probably both get pulled in."

"I don't want to catch a whale!"

"Well, you should have told me that before I bought all this whale bait!"

Dad poked her in the side, making her giggle.

Something tugged the line, causing Max to perk his ears.

Olivia panicked. "What do I do?!"

"Reel!"

Dad helped her reel in the fishing line until out popped a small silver fish. It flicked back and forth in the air, attempting to free itself from the hook. "Look at that! You caught a little trout. Good job, kid!"

Olivia smiled. She felt proud, not for catching the fish, but because she had made her father proud. She watched as he removed the hook from the fish's mouth and placed it on the dock. Max crawled forward, batting a paw at it before being swatted away. The fish thumped its tail against the wood, opening and closing its mouth in vain, unable to breathe. Olivia swore it was staring directly at her. He looked sad, like he knew what was to come. Right as she was about to speak up, her father pulled out a knife, and, in one swift motion, he cut off the fish's head. Its tail flapped twice before its headless body went limp.

Olivia couldn't breathe. A rush of heat rose into her cheeks. She didn't want to disappoint her father, but she couldn't contain herself. She began to cry.

"Hey! Hey! It's okay. Come here." Dad wrapped his arms around her. "What's wrong?"

"It . . . died," she sniffled, "because of me!"

"No, honey, the fish didn't die because of you. I'm the one who killed it. But you know what? He was going to die one day anyway. We were only trying to give his death meaning."

This didn't console Olivia one bit. "By eating him? That doesn't seem fair."

"Well, death isn't always fair, but you can choose to find meaning in it, or you can be angry about it. It will still get us one way or another."

Olivia thought for a moment as she wiped away the tears and snot dripping down her face. "But not you, right? You beat it. You're not going to die."

"One day I will, but not for a long time! I got an extension because no one else wanted to keep an eye on this little brat!" Dad messed up her hair before wrapping his arm around her again.

As it would turn out, her father was right about one thing. Death isn't always fair.

"Olivia?" Newen's voice startled her.

A heavy, cold mist floated on top of the water.

"Did I—?" Olivia didn't need to finish the sentence. Newen nodded.

Olivia felt hot and embarrassed, unable to hide her emotions even in a dream. "Sorry."

Checking that Ruda and Diego were still asleep, she crawled closer to Newen, careful not to rock the boat. She studied the puma's large golden face in the moonlight. She recognized something there in his eyes, something she'd felt many times but tried to bury. She felt like digging up that feeling now.

"Newen? Can I talk to you . . . about my dad?" she asked. It was the first time she had willingly started the conversation herself. It felt scary but good. Olivia waited for Newen to acknowledge her with one slow nod before continuing. "Well, he had cancer."

"Cancer?" asked Newen.

"Yeah, it's like the worst disease you can get. It was killing him. But then, almost magically, he was getting better. The treatments were working. We started to have hope again. We even went out to celebrate, and he started doing normal things again. We played soccer and started going on family bike rides again. It felt like I had my dad back! But then one day, out of nowhere, he just . . . didn't wake up. We still don't know why. Ma didn't want to . . . I mean, I get it. Knowing wouldn't bring him back, but it's like she didn't even . . . how could she not care." Olivia looked up at the puma, who showed no emotion but was listening intently. "I'm only telling you this because you must know what it feels like. How unfair death can be."

"Death is neither fair nor unfair. It is a natural part of life. We cannot choose when it is our time to go, nor the time for those we love."

"Yes, but—" Olivia paused. His response almost fooled her, but his tone gave him away. It was the same one she herself had used a hundred times when relatives asked her how she was doing. A quick, rehearsed *I'm fine* and a tepid smile would satisfy most of them, who'd pat her head and scamper off, having successfully checked up on her.

"You're allowed to have feelings, Newen. I mean, you seem sad, or maybe even a little guilty? You can tell me. I know how it feels."

"Hmmm." There was a long pause in which Newen continued to gaze out to the lake. "It is true. Sometimes, I think of things I should have done. Things that could have been. Things I'll never see again. But thinking of those things will not change the past. It will not bring them back."

"Like your mother?"

He turned to look at her, his eyes glowing green-gold. "She's one of them, yes."

"I feel that way too, about my dad. Maybe it was something we did together. Maybe we shouldn't have gone on that bike ride the day before. What if it was too hard for him? Or maybe if I hadn't slept over at Jill's that night, maybe I could have saved him somehow. Maybe he would still be alive. Maybe—"

Olivia's cheeks and hands began to burn. She dipped her fingers into the lake again, letting the cold water soothe her for a moment before continuing. "I don't tell anyone that, because when they see that I'm sad they all say the same thing. They say I should be happy that he's in Heaven with the angels. But that doesn't make me feel happy. It makes me angry. The angels don't need him, I need him!" Butterflies swarmed her stomach. She had never said any of this out loud before.

"Do you think I'm a bad person for thinking that?" she asked softly.

"Heaven?" asked Newen, ignoring her question. "Where is that?"

"Oh . . . it's, um . . . well . . . " She hadn't considered that Newen wouldn't know about Heaven, and quickly thought through the best way of explaining it to a puma. Not wanting to go into all that tricky water-into-wine stuff, Olivia shrugged and pointed to the sky. "Heaven is up there, I guess."

"You believe your father is in the sky?" Newen asked, his snout pointing upward. "Hmmm. You're right, I suppose. A little piece of him will always be up there, with all the stars in the sky."

Olivia gazed at the thousands of dots of light blinking on the black curtain of space, imagining one of them to be her dad. "You mean his Energy?"

"Yes. Energy can never really die. It is transformed. Even now, I can feel my mother's Energy radiating throughout this forest, in every tree, in the soil, in the water. I can feel little pieces of her everywhere.

Can you not feel your father's Energy running through you? Can you not feel him in the air you breathe and the water you drink?"

Olivia thought for a moment. It was true that she had felt Dad's presence here in some shape or form almost the entire time, but she hadn't realized it until now. He had been here from the beginning, helping her find her way when she was lost, pushing her forward throughout this entire adventure.

She then remembered his words about death. *"You can choose to find meaning in it, or you can be angry about it."* She was doing a lot of the latter lately. Choosing anger. Maybe Newen's way was better.

Still, she was curious. She pressed harder.

"But even feeling her here, do you still miss her?"

"Yes."

"Does it ever get easier?"

Newen paused once more. "It comes and goes in waves. Some days I can feel her so strongly, and she brings me joy. Other days I can't feel her anywhere. I can hardly remember her face, her voice. It's like she's slipping away. I feel very alone on these days."

Olivia frowned. "But you have Ruda! Why don't you talk to her about this?"

"It isn't her burden to bear."

"Yeah, but you don't have to—"

Olivia stopped short. She was going to say, *"You don't have to carry it all by yourself. You can ask for help."* But who was she to give him this advice when she had shut everyone out? She had tried so hard not to be a damsel in distress that she never stopped to ask herself what being a hero really meant. She had always thought that it meant doing everything yourself and never asking anyone for help, but she was starting to think she might be very wrong. Maybe real heroes were smart enough to know when to ask for help. And maybe they also knew when to offer help to those who never asked for it.

She scooted closer to the puma and rested her head against his chest, pressing her face into his fur.

"You're not alone," she said.

This was all that she could offer him in this moment, but maybe it was all he needed.

He wrapped his paw around her, pulling her in closer. His wet sandpaper tongue ran across her hair twice before his soft chin rested against her head.

As Olivia sank into his warm fur, she realized something. This whole time she was trying to make Newen feel better, she had begun to feel a little better as well. What she had told him was true. He wasn't alone. And for the first time, she realized that neither was she.

With a small weight lifted, Olivia fell asleep in a warm bed of fur for the second night in a row.

15.

HEART OF THE FOREST

A THUD JOLTED Olivia awake. Through the hazy grays of the morning's first light, she could see that they had reached the shore.

"You never woke me up," she said, stretching her neck.

"You needed your rest," said Newen. He stepped out of the boat, rocking it sideways and toppling over Diego.

"*Gusano*, get off me!" he squealed, swatting at his clothes as if he were covered in ants. He opened his eyes, startled. "Oh, we're here?"

"Yes," replied Newen.

"Woah!" Diego yelled, pointing above the tree line.

There it was, looming overhead, that jagged white cone Olivia had seen in her guidebook. It appeared much larger than she expected.

Before moving on, Newen made sure that Olivia and Diego drank water from the lake and ate enough berries and nalca to fuel themselves for the next leg of their journey.

Newen was waiting for them to finish, licking his front paw clean. "Remember, eyes and ears open," he said. "This isn't our territory anymore."

"Brumas?" asked Diego, thrusting his hand into his sling-shot-bearing pocket.

"Yes. Or worse." Ruda lowered her back and silently sprinted ahead.

Diego eyed Olivia. "You ready?"

She nodded.

They trekked upward at a steady pace, Ruda in the lead and Newen at the rear, making sure no one fell behind. The farther they went, the steeper the climb. Though the air was crisp, Olivia's body temperature spiked, her cheeks burning, and her shoulders wet with sweat. She wished that she could have bottled up some of the lake to take with them, as she'd give anything for one more sip of the icy cold water. It had only been a few months since she quit soccer, but she felt extremely out of shape. Her thighs ached with each footfall, and her breathing was long and labored.

Ruda stopped. She turned to the others, ears back and eyes wide—an unspoken warning that they were close. Lowering her body to the ground, she prowled as if on the hunt. Olivia swallowed her heavy breathing and tiptoed forward, attempting to make as little sound as humanly possible. *Humanly* being the key word, as each of her heavy steps felt clumsy compared to the animals' smooth and silent strides.

The closer they got to the so-called Heart of the Forest, the brighter everything glowed. Senses at full alert, Olivia picked up two other faint sounds. One, the sound of trickling water, which made sense since Maqui had said the Heart was surrounded by a pond. Two, the trees' whispers. They were back, but instead of a random assortment of words like before, it sounded as if hundreds of different voices were harmoniously singing together. They were still speaking some strange language, if it even was a language. It was kind of like the Hindu music Ma played during yoga, with peaceful humming sounds like *oms* and *ahs* and *ras*. Olivia stepped closer, completely transfixed by the most beautiful song she'd ever heard. The closer they came, the louder the trees' symphony soared.

Ruda paused once more before dashing behind a large tree. The others followed, all four peeking out to the side. Olivia gripped the edge of a fern blocking their view, pulling downward.

The view was spectacular. The trees were sparkling as if they'd been strung with thousands of tiny Christmas lights. They shot into the roots of hundreds of trees converging here. The roots wove in and out and around each other, creating a spiderweb with little pools of water filling in the cracks. In the very center of the space, the roots shot upward into a column. At the top of this column, the roots wove themselves into a large round ball. The longer Olivia stared at it, the more she could swear that it was actually *beating*.

Olivia swallowed her awe. She did not dare utter a single gasp. She needed to focus on their mission—get the berry safely into the center of the Heart. She scanned the clearing. Besides the trees' humming and the slow beat of the Heart, all was silent and still. There was no sign of any other presence nearby.

"They are here," whispered Newen. "Waiting."

"Well, their wait's over," said Olivia, inhaling a long breath. "Everyone ready?"

"We've got this," said Diego. "You do your thing."

Newen and Ruda nodded in unison.

As Olivia looked at her companions, she could feel the weight of their faith in her. For the first time, it didn't scare her. It made her feel strong. Their confidence fed the fire of her own, calming her, slowing her heartbeat. She was ready.

She nodded back.

"Alright," said Diego. "Here goes!"

He pushed past the fern, jumping out from their hiding spot. Diego stood, exposed, anticipating a swift downpour of Brumas from above. The trees stopped their singing, as if they too expected something bad to happen. But nothing did.

Olivia had already begun her breathing exercises, not wasting any time. She could already feel the warm mug of hot chocolate between her fingers. She was sitting on the couch, wrapped in her favorite blanket, but, this time, the movie on TV was different. It was a choose-your-own-adventure style movie, and she knew that she was the one who controlled what happened next.

Diego took one cautious step forward, then another. He craned his neck to peer into the canopy of trees. There was no sign of life anywhere.

Taking a deep breath, he yelled, "Ready or not, here I come!"

Diego sprinted in a straight and steady path along one of the larger roots stretching out from the center. When he was two paces away, a dense grey mist swept in. The trees' glowing lights turned bright red. Within this infernal mist, a thousand smoking feathers beat. They were all closing in on Diego.

Olivia was ready, willing the wind to descend from the sky. It crashed into the ground around Diego, sucking up dirt and rocks and twigs and the Brumas themselves, swirling everything around in a tornado of grey and black and red. Olivia forced this whirlwind to grow stronger, faster, fiercer, hoping to pulverize anything in its path. She could no longer see them, but she could hear them, desperately fighting to escape the raging wind. Their screeches grew louder and louder before crescendoing into a glass-shattering shriek. A burst of black shot out and sped away into the depths of the forest as the shrieking died away.

Olivia maintained the tornado's strength until Newen nudged her shoulder with his nose. She allowed the wind to calm, making sure to keep it spinning in its perfect circle around Diego. When it was nothing more than a soft breeze, the Heart of the Forest came back into view.

A scattering of dead Brumas formed a ring around Diego. He stood shell-shocked—eyes wide, mouth agape, and hair standing on end.

"That. Was. INSANE!"

He teetered to the ground, resting his back against the glowing pillar of roots slowly returning to their soft white color.

And that hadn't even been the main event; it was only a decoy to distract the Brumas. It was risky, but it had worked. Now it was Olivia's turn. As she was about to take a step out to join Diego, something tugged on the back of her jacket.

"They may come back," said Ruda. "Just in case, I'll take it. Watch my back."

Pulling out the pouch of marbles from her pocket, Olivia reached inside to collect the glowing berry. She handed it to Ruda, who nestled it into her cheek. The vixen then lowered her body and pranced into the clearing. Unlike Diego, she chose a zig-zag path, hopping gracefully from root to root over the small pools of water between them.

About halfway there, she stopped abruptly. Lowering her head, she sniffed the ground. Her tail curled inward and the hair on her back stood on edge. Something was wrong. She took one tiny hop forward, and then it happened.

A small puff of black and brown fur shot out from the opposite end of the clearing, sprinting straight for Ruda. The vixen braced herself as the spotted creature landed on top of her, digging its teeth into the top of Ruda's neck. She squealed, dropping the berry from her mouth and rolling onto her back, throwing the attacker off.

Newen leaped out from behind the tree, releasing a booming guttural growl. The attacker turned, sizing up the puma. Olivia squinted. It was that little kodkod cat, Boldo, the angry one. But how did he get here so quickly? In one swift motion, he dipped his head to collect the berry that Ruda had dropped. In a blink, he disappeared into the forest.

"No!" screamed Ruda before darting into the forest behind him.

At the same moment, a low hum announced the return of the Brumas. They filled the space with patches of gray swirls here and there. They were fewer now, Olivia having wiped out at least half, but this time they were joined by one so large, it soared overhead like a shadow blocking out the sun. Its outstretched wings rained down a gray mist on top of them, making it difficult to see. It must be another condor, like the one Olivia had taken out last time, but this one appeared even more massive.

"Protect Diego!" Newen called to Olivia before chasing after Ruda into the forest.

Olivia's heart raced. She looked for Diego but couldn't find him anywhere. The smaller Brumas had changed their pattern, no longer circling around their target in their typical fashion. Without being able to pinpoint Diego's location, there was no way Olivia could create her whirlwind without risking her friend's own safety. It seemed that the Brumas had learned from their last encounter, *evolved* even.

"Diego, where are you?" she yelled.

There was no response.

Olivia sent a strong gust of wind barreling into the Brumas, creating an opening in their mist for a few seconds. She could finally see Diego. He was at the back of the clearing and appeared to be walking into the forest. The giant Bruma followed above, its gray and black mist pouring down.

"Diego, stop!"

But he had already disappeared, leaving Olivia alone in a place which only seconds ago had been a chaotic mess. For a moment, she felt paralyzed as she tried to process what had happened. Snapping out of it, she darted after them, jumping over the puddles of water between the roots. Soon she reached the thicket of bushes and trees where Diego had disappeared. The Bruma's screeching could still be heard. Now closing in on them, Olivia saw their trail of darkness blocking out the forest's glowing lights.

Olivia followed their shadow through the woods, emerging into a narrow valley with a river cutting through the middle. It raged downward, crashing into boulders before plunging over a cliff. The wind whipped into the descending water, spraying a frothy white mist into the air. It was a waterfall, mesmerizing and mighty and most definitely deadly. And Diego was standing at its edge.

"Diego!"

She could barely see him through the patches of gray. The few smaller Brumas continued to zig-zag around him, with the mammoth still gliding ever so slowly above. Olivia took a step forward. Diego took a step backward. His eyes were wide with fear.

"Diego, stop!"

"Leave me alone!"

Olivia quickly ran through her options. She could either create more wind to blow away the Brumas and risk sending Diego over the edge or attempt to talk him out of whatever terrible nightmare he was seeing. She had no choice. She had to choose the latter.

"Diego. Whatever you're seeing is not real."

She took another step forward. Diego took another step back.

"Don't come any closer!" he yelled.

"Diego, it's me. Olivia. Remember me? I'm your friend. I'm not going to hurt you. I need you to trust me right now, okay? I need you to close your eyes and listen."

Diego shook his head. He was dangerously close to the edge at this point. His next step may be his last.

A burst of wind sent Olivia's hair flying. Tucu the owl had arrived. He flew over Diego before making a sharp turn downward with his talons extended. He grabbed two small Brumas, shook them, and then flung them into the abyss. Twisting around, he grabbed two more before the giant condor swooped in on him. He dodged it and flew back into the forest, the condor chasing after him. Diego watched, confused.

Olivia took advantage of this distraction to take several strides forward.

"Diego, close your eyes and listen to me. Don't move."

Reluctantly, he obeyed. Olivia took three more steps.

"Don't you remember me? I taught you to play marbles, and you taught me how to use your slingshot. You followed me into this strange forest and saved me from the storm. Remember that?"

Olivia was only a few feet away from him when Tucu reappeared, taking out more Brumas. But Olivia couldn't wait any longer.

"We met Newen and Ruda and Tucu and so many other animals. Don't you remember them? We're your friends. And we need you. I need you. You're the first person who hasn't made me feel like I was broken."

Diego frowned. "Olivia?"

"Yes! Yes! It's me."

Olivia held out her right hand. She was only a fingertip's distance away. There were only two bat-sized Brumas left, and Tucu was hot on their trail. She had to take the chance.

As Olivia reached for Diego's hand, the condor shot back into view. It struck Tucu, ripping into his right wing with its large talons. Tucu screeched, fighting desperately to free himself from the condor's claws. Somewhere in the struggle, the two birds lost control of their wings and both plummeted out of view.

Swallowing her scream, Olivia closed her fingers tightly around Diego's hand as he turned to peer over the cliff's edge. After a moment, he turned back to Olivia. The look in his eyes told her that he was now fully back. With a sigh, Olivia relaxed her grip. But then something happened that she didn't expect. Diego took one misstep. His ankle twisted, and he rocked his weight backwards to counterbalance. By the time he realized his mistake, it was too late.

Olivia squeezed his hand, bracing herself.

16.
CLIFF'S EDGE

THE WATERFALL'S COLD mist sprayed onto Olivia's face as her feet were pulled out from under her. She plummeted headfirst over the cliff, her stomach floating into her chest. Reaching backward, she blindly caught a small piece of rock, barely enough to hold onto.

Olivia swung sideways and crashed into the cliffside. Below her, Diego clung to her left wrist, his legs flailing as he struggled to steady himself. To her left, the waterfall's powerful stream crashed into a small pond far below. It was too far down, too small, and surrounded by too many jagged rocks. They wouldn't survive the fall.

The only way out of this situation was to climb back up, but Olivia didn't know if she had the strength. At least not the physical strength. Olivia closed her eyes, gritted her teeth, and tried to think of her mantra. The pain made it nearly impossible to concentrate, as the rock was cutting into her right hand, and her left arm felt like it might rip off at any moment, taking Diego down with it.

Focus, focus. Olivia tried to stay calm, tried to ignore the fact that both their lives depended on her. She conjured up a mental image of herself on the couch holding a mug, but her fingers were jittering. A few drops of the hot liquid splashed out, scalding her hands. Her nerves were even affecting her subconscious. Olivia breathed slower, forcing her jaw to unclench, trying to relax the muscles of her neck. She inhaled deeply, trying to block out the constant rush of water until it faded into white noise. *Now or never,* Olivia exhaled.

A burst of wind shot up from below, pushing her body up. Diego swung sideways, screaming. Just before he entered the waterfall's thick mist, he swung back. Their hands wet with mist and sweat, Olivia's grip began to slip. She panicked. She had made a huge mistake, and it might cost Diego his life. There was nothing else she could do now but pray for a miracle.

As if hearing her silent prayer, Tucu reemerged, the feathers on his checkered wings frazzled, pointing this way and that.

"Hold on," he shouted before taking a sharp turn and shooting out of view.

Olivia was extremely relieved to see that Tucu survived his fight with the condor, but she couldn't help grimacing at his command to hold on. What else could she do? Diego's face was now bright red, his large brown eyes pleading *don't let me go.* Gritting her teeth, Olivia squeezed harder, digging her fingernails into his skin. He yelped. She knew it hurt, but she didn't have a choice. She wasn't sure how much longer she could hold on.

After minutes that felt like hours, something tugged at the sleeve of Olivia's jacket. She was lifted a full foot into the air and then stopped. Her body swayed, crashing against the rock surface behind her. She checked her grip on Diego before feeling herself lifted in a quick burst, swaying and striking the rock once more. For the third time, she was lifted until she was finally over the top of the cliff.

Her body was dragged along the rocky soil, pulling Diego behind her until he too was on solid ground. Olivia loosened her grip on him and ran her fingers across the rocky soil she lay on. Solid ground.

A large snout came into view overhead, lowering itself to draw a long, wet lick across her cheek. Newen's emerald eyes peered down at her.

"Are you alright?" asked the puma.

Olivia sat up, dizzy. "Yes. Diego?"

"I'm okay," Diego wheezed, resting back against Newen's side.

Newen licked the boy's hair as if he were bathing a kitten. And Diego did look like a scared kitten, small and fragile, propped up by the large cat. He pulled his knees to his chest, his trembling hands wrapping around them. Olivia could hardly recognize this haunted version of the happy-go-lucky boy she'd first met. *What did Diego see that frightened him so much?*

Olivia crawled over, gently touching Diego's shoulder. "Hey, you know you're safe now, right?"

Diego smiled weakly. "Yeah, thanks to you. You saved my life. I don't think . . . I would've—" His watery eyes exposed all of the emotions that he could not put into words.

"Hey, come on!" Olivia cut him off. "It's no big deal. I owed you one anyway. Now we're even." She gently punched his shoulder.

With an unconvincing smile and not a single joke to counter, Diego slumped back against Newen's side. His trembling subsided, but he still looked weak.

"Do you—" Olivia hesitated. She hated this question, the one she had been asked a thousand times. But she knew it needed to be said. "Do you want to talk about it?"

Diego closed his eyes, exhaling heavily. Olivia waited. After a minute, he spoke.

"There's a reason I like walking around with don Pancho in the forest. Or anywhere, really, as long as it's not my house."

He paused. Olivia considered how much she should ask, but she didn't want to pry. So she waited.

"It's—" He stopped. "Wait, where's Ruda?"

Newen motioned his head toward the volcano. "I didn't catch her in time."

"What do you mean?!"

"She was chasing Boldo and crossed into Kutral's territory. He has her. And the canelo berry."

"WHAT?" Olivia and Diego shouted in unison.

"How can you sit there listening to me whine when Ruda's in danger?" Diego accused.

"He won't hurt her," replied Newen calmly. "And you needed some time to recover."

"How do you know that?" asked Olivia. "How do you know that he won't hurt her?"

"Kutral has never intentionally harmed an animal," said Tucu, perched on a branch above them. He was plucking out his damaged feathers, creating a bald patch on the inside of his right wing.

"Then why does he even want her?" asked Olivia.

"He doesn't want *her*," answered Tucu.

Newen looked away. It wasn't long before Olivia connected the dots. He only wanted the humans. He was only using Ruda to get to them.

"Well . . . so what? We can't leave her there." Diego stood, wobbling a bit before regaining his balance.

"This isn't your fight," said Newen. "It's dangerous."

"I don't care how dangerous it is. I don't care how many of those stupid Brumas I have to walk through to get there. We need to rescue her. She would do the same for us. Right Olivia?"

Olivia stood and nodded. "Let's go get her."

Newen sighed. "I thought you may say that." He stood, stretching his front paws quickly before walking over and whispering in Tucu's ear. The owl nodded and promptly took flight. By now Olivia was all too used to the owl's comings and goings, but she wondered what his mission was this time.

"So!" Diego turned to Newen. "How fast can you run?"

17.
THE VOLCANO

NEWEN SPRINTED THROUGH the forest as Olivia clung to his thick fur for dear life, and Diego clung to Olivia's waist for *his* dear life. Each one of the puma's long strides threw the children into the air, leaving them weightless before crashing down with a thud. Wind rushing into her face, Olivia felt as if she were flying. She imagined this must be what riding a horse was like, something she had always wanted to do. And now here she was, not riding a horse but a puma. Had it not been for the dangerous mission ahead, she would have enjoyed it.

They climbed higher, leaving the lush green landscape behind. The trees became shorter, thinner, sparser, and the soil turned from a rich brown to dusty gray. Soon, not a single tree remained, and there was nothing but rocky gray soil. It looked like the surface of the moon.

Newen slowed, treading forward cautiously, his breathing labored from the run. Ahead of them, a shimmering energy field shot into the sky. Beyond this, the ground dipped into a large crater with soil as red as blood. Although the volcano's snow-covered peak was still high above them, Olivia knew that they had arrived.

Before Newen could take another step, a small brown and black cat shot out of the crater and sprinted toward them. He stopped right before crossing the shimmering barrier. Boldo.

"Welcome to—"

"Traitor!" Newen roared.

"As rude as ever, Newen," said Boldo. He cleared his high-pitched voice and continued. "Welcome to Kutral's domain! Please announce yourselves and the reason for your visit."

"He knows who we are and why we're here."

"Yeah!" shouted Diego. "We're here for Ruda! Give her back!"

"Very well, I will inform him that two dirty humans and one large chicken are here to—"

"Stop the games, Boldo," boomed Newen. "Let me speak with my brother."

Brother. The word bounced around Olivia's head, connecting the missing pieces of the puzzle. Newen's mysterious guilt now made sense. She slid off of the puma's back, turning to face him.

"Why didn't you tell us?" she asked.

A look of shame washed over Newen, stronger than she'd ever seen. His ears pinned back, and his furry white brows sagged. "I am sorry. I could not admit that—"

"My dear brother. How long I've waited for you," echoed a low raspy voice. A gray figure stepped out of the crater below. Its eyes glowed red, and its body emitted wisps of smoke like the dying embers of a campfire. The ground turned burnt orange everywhere its fiery feet touched.

"Hello, Newen. It's so nice to see you again, after all these years. Do you like my new look? It's *on fire*, isn't it?" He coughed out a low, devious cackle. Every sound strained out of his mouth, as if his vocal cords had been singed with the rest of him.

"I am sorry for what has become of you, brother," said Newen. "But this is your own fault."

"MY fault?" Kutral drifted closer. "Perhaps if you had helped save Mother from those *humans*, this never would have happened to me!"

"I tried!" screamed Newen.

Kutral jumped onto a large rock mere feet away from the energy field. The closer he came, the redder the barrier glowed. "You think you tried?" he spat. "Let's see exactly how much you tried."

"Kutral, NO!"

A series of moving images flashed inside Olivia's head. She was looking out from behind a large fern. Two warm brown eyes stared back at her. A soft whisper.

"Stay hidden. Don't come out. For anything."

Then she was gone.

In the dark, a loud hiss, men yelling, a gunshot.

Olivia struggled to move, but she was pinned down by a small cub with the same emerald eyes as Newen. He was fighting to keep her there.

As Olivia realized that she was seeing things from the eyes of another puma cub, the vision was gone.

"*That* is how you tried?" Kutral accused.

"She told us to stay hidden. She told us—" Newen shook his head. "I think of that night all the time. It hurts me to think of it. I wish I could have done more, but I know—I *know*—there's nothing we could have done."

"We could have fought!"

"We were too young."

"We are not young anymore, Brother. But still, you do nothing."

"Revenge will not bring her back!"

"No, perhaps it is too late for our dear Mother. We cannot have her back. But we can stop what happened to her from ever happening to any other creature again. Like your fox friend. Terrible what *their* kind has done to her."

"What do you want, Kutral?" Newen furled his nose and bared his teeth.

Kutral sneered, pacing around the rock. "You know what I want.

I don't want the fox, not one little bit. She is an innocent creature after all. Give me those *humans* and I'll let her go."

Olivia stepped forward. "Okay." She said it before she could think twice.

"Olivia, no." Newen stepped in front of her, blocking her path.

"I'll be okay," she said. "I have a plan." This was a lie, but the truth was that deep down she believed there must be some good in Kutral. She would be able to reason with him, somehow.

"What a brave little girl!" Kutral mocked. "Boldo has told me so much about you and your . . . *abilities*. I'm so excited to see what you can do!"

Diego hopped off of Newen's back, joining Olivia's side. "I'm going with her."

"Ah yes, can't forget about the other one!" Kutral joked.

"Hey, he's more than that," Olivia proclaimed, grabbing his hand.

"How touching." Kutral rolled his eyes. "Well, come along."

"Wait," said Diego. "If we follow you, do you promise you'll let Ruda go?"

"Oh yes, of course. I *promise*."

Diego clenched his fist. "Fine. Let's go."

"Good boy," Kutral snickered as he drifted back into the crater. "Oh, and by the way, Newen, if *you* step one foot across this lovely energy field you've made me, I'll kill them."

With that, Kutral vanished, leaving Newen growling at nothing but smoke.

"You heard him. In you go. One at a time," Boldo ordered, not at all hiding how much he enjoyed bossing them around.

"So you're his servant now, are you?" snarled Newen, clawing into the ground.

"Better than joining forces with the humans like you have," the little cat replied.

"They're not who you think they are."

"We'll have plenty of time to debate that later, but right now, these two need to get a move on it. Come on!"

Olivia gave one last reassuring glance to Newen before stepping through the glittering energy field. Diego followed with Boldo at his heels, ushering them toward the red crater. As they approached it, Olivia's head filled with fog. It was the same feeling she had inside the Brumas' mist. Breathing deeply, in through her nose and out through her mouth, Olivia prepared herself for what was to come.

Arriving at the mouth of the crater, they paused to peer into it. Olivia was relieved to see the bottom not too far down. She and Diego locked eyes.

"So," Diego whispered. "You have a plan?"

Olivia swallowed. "Whatever happens, remember what's real."

"Stop chattering and climb in," ordered Boldo. "You *two-leggeds* do know how to climb, don't you?"

Olivia tried her best to ignore him. She knelt and began crawling backwards, carefully selecting footholds and handholds as she went. As the brain-fog thickened, she focused on the feeling of the rocks beneath her hands, forcing herself to stay in the present.

Once she landed at the bottom, Olivia turned to inspect her surroundings. There appeared to be some sort of tunnel in the depths of the volcano. Diego landed behind her.

"Woah, a lava tube," exclaimed Diego. "I didn't know these existed here."

Of course that's what it was. Olivia couldn't help feeling a burst of disappointment for not realizing it before Diego had. She had read about lava tubes several times. During an eruption, lava could eat through layers of rock in a volcano. Once the eruption ended, the lava would drain away, leaving a long cave or tunnel like the one they were heading toward.

Olivia and Diego walked toward the mouth of the tunnel, with Boldo right behind them. Tiny cracks and holes in the ceiling allowed enough light to stream in, illuminating their path forward. As Olivia's eyes adjusted to this low light, she noticed that the ceiling was covered in icicle-like rock formations.

"Stalagmites," she whispered, eager to say it before Diego.

The tunnel seemed to have no end. Olivia wondered how far they would have to walk. She would have to stay alert the entire time, waiting for something, anything, to happen, knowing it could be at any moment. Her shoulders tensed as she imagined what might be waiting for her at the end of the tunnel.

Hissss.

Hissssssssss.

Olivia could hear it now, the same low hiss from before, the one that belonged to that *thing* with the long sharp claws. But whether it was actually here or her mind playing tricks, she didn't know. With each step, it seemed to grow a little bit louder, a little bit closer.

Diego nudged her shoulder, forcing her to look up. A jagged doorway had appeared in the rock wall on their right. They stopped, peering in. In the far corner of the cavernous room, two pairs of eyes glowed low to the ground. Before Olivia could walk closer, a large puma crossed the threshold, startling her. She didn't recognize its markings, but something about it seemed familiar. From where the puma had come, a long silver stick emerged. As Olivia inched closer, she realized it wasn't a stick. It was a rifle. Her stomach sank. She ran.

Right before she reached the opening, rocks from the ceiling crumbled down. She jumped back just in time, but now the doorway was gone.

Olivia grabbed a rock in the middle of the pile. It wouldn't budge. Placing her right foot against the pile, she kicked with all her strength. Still, nothing. It was too big, too stuck, and too much for her.

"Help me!" yelled Olivia. "We can't—"

A metallic bang echoed out from the other side, followed by a dull thump. Olivia froze, staring at the pile of rocks until she felt a hand squeeze her shoulder.

"Let go, Olivia," said Diego. "It's not real, remember?"

"Not real, eh?" asked Boldo. "Seemed pretty real to me."

Olivia released her grip on the rock. Her palms were red and dotted with hundreds of tiny puncture wounds. The pain reminded her that, although what she saw may be fake, the consequences were very real. She would need to calm herself. They were only at the beginning, and she knew that the worst was to come.

"Keep moving," demanded Boldo after a few seconds.

The tunnel stretched out for a seemingly infinite length until a new door appeared, a regular wooden door built into the rock wall. A series of rapid *pop-pop-pops* resounded from within, where a teenage boy sat in a wooden chair that was much too small for him. He had long black hair down to his shoulders and the hint of a moustache under his long pointy nose. He held a slingshot in his hands from which he launched small pebbles against the wall. Stopping mid-fling, he turned to look at them. His eyes lit up with devilish delight as he stared directly at Diego.

"Oh, hey, runt! Look what I found." He waved around the slingshot. "I figured you don't need it since you've got no friends to play with anyway."

Diego reached for Olivia's hand and squeezed. "I do too," he whispered.

"Speak up now, runt."

Diego looked up and proclaimed, "I said, I DO have friends!"

The teenager chuckled. "You mean that crazy old man who goes out lookin' for fairies and goblins in the woods?"

"He's not crazy! Show some respect!"

The teenager dropped the slingshot and shoved his hand into his front pocket. He then pulled out a brown and white striped snake, which slithered around his arm. Diego turned a pale shade of green and clutched Olivia's hand even harder.

"Did'ja hear that, Gusano?" The teenager stroked the snake's head. It flicked its tongue at him in response. "Runt here is try'na teach *us* about *respect*. Can you believe it, after the terrible way he's treated you?" The boy glared at Diego. "Maybe we oughtta teach him a lesson."

Diego stepped back, but before he could dodge him, the teenager grabbed his arm, ripping him from Olivia's grasp. She ran after her friend, but as she reached the door, it slammed closed. Screaming

Diego's name, she banged on the wood and pulled at the handle, but there was no use.

"Diego! You have to remember—"

"So sad," said Boldo. "Well, one down, one to go. Must keep going."

"You," Olivia seethed. "Why are you doing—"

Before she could finish her sentence, the hissing returned, deafening, as if it were licking at her ears. She closed her eyes and covered her ears, every fiber of her being wanting to shrink into a ball and hide. But she couldn't do that. She knew she had to confront her own nightmare. That was the only way out. Olivia took two long breaths before opening her eyes.

There it was, standing at the end of the tunnel, the same monster that had held Max in its claws. Somehow, it was even uglier than before. An acidic stench wafted down the hallway, like a piece of rotten meat had been dunked in a bucket of nail polish remover. Olivia covered her nose and mouth. The monster stood, hunched over, its jagged-toothed jaw hanging abnormally low, as if it were dislocated.

Olivia stood paralyzed, terrified but transfixed by the gruesome thing standing before her. The creature turned. Behind it, a new door appeared, painted royal blue. Hanging over the door was a pink-and-yellow flower wreath, the same wreath that hung over the door to her parents' bedroom.

The creature raised its right arm, placing its long black claws on the door handle. It began to turn.

With a sudden jolt of energy, Olivia sprinted. She would make it. She had to. But the faster she ran, the farther she was from the door, as if the hallway were extending out in front of her. The door creaked open, giving her a glimpse of the thing she most loved on the other side. She flew forward, forcing her feet to move faster. But it was no use. The doorway grew smaller and smaller. The monster crept inside. It gave Olivia one last look at its hideous snarl before slamming the door shut.

Olivia continued to run toward the door in a blind frenzy. A moment too late, she realized that the hallway had stopped growing. She collided with the blue wood at full speed, the force of the blow throwing her backwards. She rolled to her side, cradling her knees as sharp pain flew down her spine.

"Oh my," said Boldo. "I don't know why you want to be in there with that thing. Why, I'd *die* of fright."

Her pain intensifying her anger, Olivia had a sudden desire to strangle this rude little cat and shut him up for good. But before she could lift herself off the ground, another sound caught her attention. It was coming from the room next door. *Her* room. She stood, still dizzy from the crash, and staggered forward until she reached the doorframe. Peering around the corner, she held her breath.

Everything appeared almost exactly as it was before, except dimmer and duller, as if something had sucked the light out. The sky-blue walls were now a stormy shade of gray, and the sponged-on animal-shaped clouds seemed to droop in defeat.

The curtains had been pulled shut on all the windows but one, at which her mother stood. She was swaying back and forth, humming her favorite song.

Every few seconds she pulled a piece of clothing out of a drawer in Olivia's dresser and placed it in one of two cardboard boxes labeled *Chile* and *Donate*. Olivia hobbled over to her, grabbing her mother's arm.

"Stop it!" she screamed. "He isn't even . . . you can't . . . you have to do something!"

But Ma only continued humming and swaying as she packed away Olivia's life-long possessions. Olivia stepped to her left, now face-to-face with her mother. Only then could she see that below the woman's lifeless eyes appeared to be what could only be described as a *smile*.

Of course she was smiling. Even now, she was still *Peppy Pepa*.

Olivia's anger was taking over her entire body, making her insides burn, twisting and churning inside of her like molten lava. The heat became so intense that she could feel the toxic gases bubbling inside

of her, ready to explode. The dim lights of energy running through Olivia's hands burned bright, shifting colors from white to gold to fluorescent orange. They grew more intense until she was smoldering crimson red.

The walls around her shook. The floor swayed below her feet.

"Olivia!" A voice called from somewhere, a voice she once knew. "Remember what's real!"

Remember what's real? This is real. Ma had given up, exactly like this. She had painted on that hideous smile and packed up their entire life and moved to the opposite end of the Earth. She did all this, despite having just lost the man she loved. Olivia reeled with disgust.

She could hear the hissing growing stronger from the room next door, her parent's room. It sounded different now, less like a hiss and more like a vacuum sucking in air. Olivia panicked. It was almost too late. Desperate, she shook her mother by the shoulders, hard. Still, she did not react.

The hissing crescendoed, then stopped suddenly. Everything went silent except for the pounding in Olivia's ears. She didn't need to see it to know what had happened. It was done. Over. He was gone.

Olivia dug her nails into her palms as she looked at the zombie-like woman standing next to her.

"This is your fault." She grabbed her mother's arms and squeezed. "You didn't care enough. You didn't even try!"

Her fingers continued to press into her mother's skin. Not once did the woman flinch. Not once did she react.

Lava boiled under Olivia's skin. Unable to contain it any longer, she closed her eyes and screamed, releasing her burning, red-hot rage.

The ground shook harder and harder. The windows rattled louder and louder. A low rumbling grew stronger and stronger until the walls crumbled all around her.

18.

DEAD-END

"YOUR ANGER IS quite impressive." The voice pierced Olivia's ears, breaking her concentration.

The sponged-on clouds of her old bedroom were gone, replaced by the jagged rock walls of the volcanic tunnel. This time, those same walls no longer stretched out an infinite length in front of her. Instead, they curled inward, transforming into a crypt-like cave. This was it. The end of the tunnel, a dead-end.

A stream of sunlight splashed onto the ground in front of her, pouring in from a round opening at the very top of a dome high above. Olivia reasoned that this must be where, who knows how many years ago, the lava had melted through the rock and formed the very tunnel in which she stood. Had this been any other time, she would have marveled at such unexpected beauty in such a dark place.

At the far end of the cave, a dark figure slowly paced, never fully entering the ring of light in the center. *Kutral.* Olivia followed his silhouette with her eyes, refusing to let him out of her sight.

"When Boldo told me about your power," Kutral's brittle voice cracked, "I never imagined it could be so *explosive*."

As if on cue, a large boulder came tumbling down from above, crashing into a pile of rocks a few feet away. One small pebble ricocheted off the wall, landing at Olivia's feet. Instead of coming to a stop, it vibrated against the ground. Everything was shaking.

Olivia shook her head. She couldn't ignore what she had done, what her anger had done. The same anger that, even now, she could feel twisting her insides into a feverish knot.

A series of footsteps grew louder behind her.

"Where's Ruda?" Diego demanded.

"Ah, here he comes," Kutral purred. "Boldo, could you not contain him?"

"I'm sorry, Kutral," Boldo coughed, out of breath. "I tried, but he—"

"Enough," Kutral interrupted. "We're all here now, I suppose."

"So let her go," yelled Diego with even more force. "That was the deal."

"It was, wasn't it?" teased Kutral. His glowing red eyes shifted to the left and vanished in the dark. Olivia followed the wisps of smoke seeping off his body as he rounded the edge of the cave, drawing closer to them. Several seconds passed before he stopped, mere feet away. "She's only right over there." He pointed his snout to the right. "Fell into a hole, poor thing."

Diego and Olivia sprinted toward the light in the middle of the cave. There, they found her, hopping up and down in a shallow pit, clawing at the dirt wall with her one front paw to no avail.

"Ruda!" shouted Diego.

"Olivia, Diego!" exclaimed Ruda, leaping higher.

The children snatched handfuls of rocks, throwing them off to the side, until there was enough space for Diego to lay against the ground. Olivia gripped his ankles as he threw his arms over the edge. Scooting forward, Diego lowered his upper body into the pit as Olivia pulled backward to support his weight.

"Big jump!" he yelled to the fox.

Ruda pushed down on her hind legs, propelling herself into Diego's arms. Olivia pulled backward, dragging them over the edge and out of the pit. She then joined in their embrace, wrapping her arms around the little fox as if she hadn't seen her in years.

"Very well," growled Kutral. "I held up my end of the bargain, and now it's time to hold up yours. Say goodbye."

Ruda looked back and forth between the two children and Kutral. "Oh no . . . no no no! You two turned yourself in to Kutral? For ME? No no no no no NO!"

"Ruda, it was our choice," said Diego.

Ruda squinted suspiciously. "Well, then I'm not leaving." She plopped her backside firmly on the ground.

Olivia finally found the strength to speak. "Ruda, you have to go back to Newen. You have to trust us."

The vixen shifted her eyes from Olivia to Diego, then back to where Kutral's two red eyes glowed.

"No," she repeated, as defiant as ever.

"So you'd like to stay and watch, then, fox?" hissed Kutral. "Perhaps we'll do the same to them as was done to you. Interesting to see what happens when a two-legged becomes a one-legged, no?" He coughed out another laugh.

Ruda's scruff stood on end.

"But," continued Kutral, "if you leave now, I may leave them in one piece."

"I swear, if you even—"

"Oh, no, I promise! I only want to chat." Kutral's voice dissolved into a soothing syrup. "Boldo, shall we escort our fox friend out now?"

"This way, please," said Boldo, nudging Ruda forward with his head.

"Get off me!" hissed the fox. "I'll go, but let me say goodbye first."

Kutral conceded with one long nod.

As the children hugged Ruda once more, she whispered into their ears, "The canelo berry. Boldo gave it to Kutral. You must get it back!" And then, with one last angry glare at Kutral, she scampered off with Boldo behind her.

"Marvelous," said Kutral. "Now that we're alone—" He lunged toward them, into the light.

Olivia tripped backward, crashing into the ground. Diego knelt beside her, pressing a reassuring palm on her shoulder.

"Oh, there there," Kutral cooed. "Don't be afraid."

"We're not afraid of you," said Diego, standing tall. "You could have killed us already, but you haven't. Which makes you no better than a bored house cat, playing with its prey. But we're done with your games!"

"Is that so?" Kutral stepped closer to Diego, his crimson eyes burning deep into the boys' own. He lowered himself into an unmistakable attack position, but before he could pounce, Olivia closed her eyes, forcing another boulder to shake loose from the ceiling. It crashed right in front of Kutral, who stumbled backward. Olivia exhaled. It had worked, but she knew she couldn't do that again without risking the whole cave collapsing.

Kutral released a guttural growl as he paced, visibly deliberating his next course of attack. He stopped abruptly, and his expression changed. The grey smoke that swirled around his ghost-like body floated downward, descending upon Olivia and Diego. Before she could think, Olivia lunged at Diego, pushing him out of the way.

The last thing she saw was a hint of a smile on Kutral's face before the scene shifted.

Once again, she was back in her old room.

One. More. Time.

There she was, her mother, still staring out the window. Still wearing that ghostly smile. The anger Olivia had felt before swelled like a tidal wave, washing over every inch of her.

She took a step forward, fists clenched tight.

"Olivia!" echoed a voice from somewhere far away. Olivia's body swayed back and forth, as if an invisible force were tugging at her. "It's not real," said the same voice. "Whatever it is you're seeing, remember that it's not real!"

"No," she whispered, staring at the lifeless woman before her. "This is real."

"Remember Newen and Ruda?" pleaded the voice. "THEY are real."

The names affected her somehow, like a lost memory buried deep down inside of her. She could almost remember them, but when she tried picturing their faces, it was like they were standing behind a layer of fog.

A low noise broke her concentration. Ma had begun to hum that song once again, the flat one that crept under Olivia's skin, feeding the fuel of her anger.

"Remember what they taught you. Remember how to control your emotions," echoed the unseen voice.

Control your emotions, Olivia repeated to herself. The words unearthed something within her. The fog began to evaporate. Her memory became clearer. She knew what the voice, *Diego's* voice, wanted her to do, but she didn't know if she could.

Her face was burning, the muscles in her stomach clenched. Her heart pounded high in her ribcage, drumming fast and loud in her ears. She knew it was all fueled by the mixture of ugly emotions running through her. She needed to calm herself, but it felt nearly impossible.

Olivia closed her eyes, trying to remember Tucu's training. Inhaling her first long, deep breath, she retained the air for a few seconds, picturing herself holding a mug. She imagined feeling the warmth in her hands, smelling the melted chocolate float into the air. When she exhaled, she could feel her stomach releasing an ounce of tightness. Her heart's drumming grew a bit softer, slower. Inhaling once more, she imagined bringing the mug to her lips. As Olivia continued to visualize the couch, and the blanket, and Max curled up at her feet, ever so slowly, her heartbeat calmed. Eventually, the poisonous lava burning in her chest dissolved until all that was left were a few small embers of a cozy fire.

A sniffle disrupted Olivia's meditation. Ma's silhouette blocked out the light coming in from the window. Her back was turned, but even so, Olivia could tell that there was something different about her this time.

"Ma?" she whispered, stepping forward.

"Hey, honey." Ma ran her sleeve across her cheek before turning to look at Olivia. "You're home. Good. I need to talk to you."

She walked over to the bed and patted a spot next to her, indicating where her daughter should sit. Olivia obeyed. As she took a seat on the bed, she felt a sudden sense of deja vu.

Ma rubbed her cheeks once more, attempting to hide the tears that had already stained her face. "I made you a submarine. It's over there."

Olivia picked up the mug on her nightstand. It was cold, the little bar of chocolate floating lifeless in a sea of white. Had her mother forgotten to heat it up? She placed it back on the nightstand before feeling a gentle squeeze on her shoulder.

"Your father. He—" Ma paused, visibly struggling to get the words out. "He didn't wake up. I don't know how . . . they came and—" She shook her head before saying it, the most terrible words, the words that no child should ever have to hear. "Livy, honey, I'm so sorry. Dad died last night."

Only then, staring at Ma's pink eyes and splotchy cheeks, did Olivia realize that *this* was real. This had actually happened.

She then remembered what came next: an overwhelming hurricane of emotions so fast and so strong that she must have blocked out this memory completely. All she remembered was waking up the next day, at which point Ma had already put on a strong face to prepare for the funeral arrangements. Olivia had never seen another tear fall from her eyes. It was all business, then packing, then leaving, smiling all the while as if this were some fun new adventure. And Olivia had hated her for it. Blamed her even.

But now she could see the truth. Whereas Olivia had hidden her sadness beneath a layer of anger and resentment, Ma had buried hers even deeper. Beneath her back-to-business, everything's-fine, Peppy Pepa attitude, Ma had been hurting just as much as Olivia. Maybe more. With this realization came an incredible pang of guilt.

Olivia sank into Ma's arms. They were warm and comforting, like sinking into a big soft blanket on a cold winter day. It was everything she had needed yet tried so hard to push away.

"I'm sorry, too," Olivia whispered, before closing her eyes and inhaling one last deep breath.

19.
MIND GAMES

THE VISION FADED. But this time, when Olivia opened her eyes, she did not find herself back in the tunnel. Instead, it was all black nothingness. That is, except for one small creature that lay curled up in a ball in front of her.

As Olivia walked around to face it, she realized it was a puma cub. It looked so scared, with its paws curled in under its chest, shaking.

"Newen?" Olivia whispered, crouching to look closer.

The cub peeked up at her. His eyes were gold, not green like Newen's.

Get out of my head, an unseen voice echoed loudly from all around.

Olivia stood, taken aback. She scanned her surroundings once more. There was still nothing there . . . nothing visible, at least. Looking back at the small cub before her, she slowly realized where she was. Just as Kutral had managed to break into her mind, she must now, somehow, be looking into his.

She took a small step forward.

"Is this how you see yourself, still?"

For the first time, she felt pity for Kutral.

Get out! Demanded the voice.

"It's okay. I know why you feel this way. I—"

You know NOTHING, rang a voice. *It was YOUR kind that killed her.*

"I know," replied Olivia softly, unable to negate such a terrible fact. "It's not fair, and I can't undo it. All I can say in our defense is that not all humans are like that. Most of us are . . . "

The small puma cub lying at her feet transformed, growing into a large adult. He crouched down, preparing to attack. Olivia threw herself to the side and twisted back as the large cat leapt after a group of humans scattering in a frenzy. As Olivia watched Kutral sprint after them, she knew what would happen next. The attacks. The demon in the forest. It had been Kutral.

As Olivia stared into the abyss, a series of screams and gunshots rang out. Kutral returned, his snout and jaw soaked, crimson red. Olivia's stomach clenched as she wondered how many people he had slaughtered.

He walked straight past her, ignoring her. Two humans now appeared face down on the ground in front of him. They didn't move, didn't even breathe. Beside them sat a child no more than a year old. Olivia ran to the child, ready to scoop him up in her arms, but all she felt was air. He wasn't there. She should have known. This may have been real at some time, but it was now only a memory that she was witnessing. Olivia looked back at the pacing puma and held her breath.

The voice returned.

My mother's death made me realize my true purpose, to rid the world of the plague of humans so that no other innocent creature must die at your hands.

Olivia continued to wait for the puma to pounce on his prey, but he never did. He only snarled, showing his blood-soaked teeth.

The child stretched his chubby little fingers toward the puma's face, seemingly unaware of what had happened to his parents. The puma continued to pace before finally turning to leave.

Olivia exhaled, relieved. "You didn't kill the child."

No, I . . . it was worse to leave it alive, for it to know the misery of growing up without parents.

"I don't think that's why," Olivia replied softly. "I think you saw that it was innocent, which means…"

No.

"You know there's hope for us."

The child and two adults disappeared. They were replaced by another man. It was difficult to make out his face, but Olivia recognized his jacket. It was the same jacket that she was wearing.

All humans deserve to die, just as your father did.

The familiar spark of rage flared once more, faster and more intense than before. Olivia advanced toward the man, but not even two steps forward, she stopped. *This isn't real,* she reminded herself. It wasn't even a memory, it was just another lie. Whoever or whatever was on the ground wasn't her father.

Olivia now understood. Kutral's entire power was telling lies. And this lie was so in-your-face obvious that it hurt. How could she allow herself to get so angry about something she knew wasn't true? She got angry because she *chose* to believe the lies. She *chose* to be angry. But now, recognizing that it was her choice after all, she took back the power that Kutral had over her.

It was time to end this mind game. It was time to return to the real world.

The ground beneath her feet began to shake, the man on the ground dissipating in a swirl of black smoke. Her dad's old jacket was the last thing to vanish before the tunnel came into focus once more, the real Kutral stepping forward.

"Enough," said Olivia, standing tall. "I'm not going to fall for your tricks or let you make me angry anymore."

"You think I'm responsible for your anger?" Kutral sneered,

walking in a circle around Olivia and Diego.

Rocks continued to crumble and fall from the ceiling above. Olivia grabbed Diego's hand, pulling him backward. They turned, in step with Kutral, keeping their backs to the opposite wall.

"It's been there, inside you, this entire time," said Kutral. "All I did was whisper ideas into your mind. And how easy it was! You believed them without question, not because I planted them in your head, but because they had long ago begun to take root, like a weed growing uncontrolled in that hidden part of yourself, buried deep in the dark. With the smallest of suggestions, you cracked wide open, letting all of that boiled up rage erupt. No, I am not responsible for your anger. You are! And now you will also be responsible for all the damage it causes to this forest."

Olivia was stunned. As much as she hated to admit it, he was right. It hadn't been the Brumas or Kutral or some other big bad villain who caused that storm, or wiped out all those trees, or started this volcanic eruption. She had done all those things. She was the dangerous one. She had been so afraid of what demons might be hiding in the forest, she hadn't realized that the real demon was inside of her all along, clawing to get out.

Everything that Kutral had shown her about her father's death and the anger she felt toward her mother, it was how she already felt. It was an ugly truth that made her sick to her stomach. But there was no denying it now.

"You're right," Olivia said weakly. "I have been angry. It was so much easier to be angry instead of any of those other things. Sad. Hurt. Alone. But now I see that it's not right to bury all of that. Being angry only hurts people, and it hurts me too. I'm done with it now. I'm ready to start healing."

The ground stopped shaking, and the volcano's rumbling died down. It was calming. Olivia released a long breath of relief. Maybe it wasn't too late to make this right. Maybe they could still get out of here and save the forest. But for that, they would need the canelo berry. With everything else going on, she had completely forgotten about it. She had to convince Kutral to give it up, or else join them in saving the forest, no matter how impossible that seemed.

"Kutral?" Olivia still believed that there was good in him. She had to try to find it. "I know you're hurting too. I can't take that away from you, but maybe we can help each other try to heal together."

"Heal?" Kutral's dark cloud of smoke grew taller. His red eyes burned bright. "After everything you humans have done, you want me to forget it all, walk off with you, and talk about *my feelings*?"

The ground jolted once more, shaking side to side and up and down, fiercer than ever. Olivia and Diego held on to each other, struggling to maintain their balance. More and more rocks crashed from above as the sides of the cave's wall began to crack open. A trickle of neon-bright lava dripped in through the opening overhead. Olivia and Diego jumped backward.

"Stop this!" shouted Diego, urgently. "Come back with us. We can start over. All of us."

"Come back with you?" yelled Kutral. "I can't leave. My own brother trapped me here! My own *brother*!"

Kutral roared, and the ground shook harder. A large stalagmite fell from the ceiling, and Diego pulled Olivia out of the way just in time.

Olivia thought fast. They were running out of time. "You have to give us the canelo berry! We can use it to break the barrier that's keeping you here. You have to stop this and let us go. You have to trust us."

Kutral snickered. *"Trust you?"*

He crept in the opposite direction. Sniffing the ground, he scratched at the dirt, uncovering where he had buried the glowing berry.

"You thought you could save the forest with this little thing?" Kutral placed his claw on top of it and pressed down, piercing its core. Its glowing light blinked like a dying lightbulb.

"No!" shouted Olivia. "Stop!"

"Pathetic," scoffed Kutral, lifting his paw off the berry. It was still blinking, barely. "You humans have been destroying the forest for years, and you think something this small can save it? Face it. This is the end. The forest is dying, and the only thing left to do is make sure *you* die with us!"

Kutral's eyes blazed with fire as he pushed off with his back legs, leaping toward them. Olivia ducked and rolled to the left, out of his reach.

Diego reacted one second too slow.

Kutral's teeth tore into his right leg. Diego screamed so high it made Olivia's stomach churn.

"Stop!" Olivia called out, but the puma was already moving backward, dragging Diego with him. "Let him go!"

Olivia ran toward them, causing Kutral to bite down harder. Diego let out another scream of agony.

Olivia stopped dead in her tracks, heart pounding. She needed to think, quick. Perhaps there was something here she could use. Her gaze landed back on Diego. In his left hand, he held his slingshot by his side. He tossed it out as far as he could. It landed a short distance from the canelo berry. Glancing up at Kutral, Olivia quickly gaged the distance between them. She could make it.

Kutral released his grip on Diego's leg. "Another one of your human weapons?"

He lowered his body to pounce, but Olivia was ready. She bolted toward the slingshot.

She grabbed it with her right hand and swiped the berry with her left, then reached into her pocket and swapped the berry for a marble.

Just in time, she rolled sideways, dodging Kutral's long claws. Leaping to her feet, she placed the marble in the sling. She pulled back as hard as she could, exactly as Diego had taught her. She aimed directly at Kutral, held her breath, and then let go.

Kutral threw back his head, roaring in pain. His gray smoke

turned bright red, matching the lava, which dripped at an alarming rate. Olivia had hit him right in the eye. She watched, horrified, as Kutral pawed at his face, flinching as more rocks crashed down around him. He didn't deserve this, no matter how bad he was. He could have changed and—

"Olivia, we need to go . . . NOW!" shouted Diego, still on the ground, his leg bleeding.

Olivia ran to Diego and placed her arm under his shoulder. Pulling him up, she began dragging him as fast as she could back into the tunnel. Diego leaned on Olivia, trying to use his one good leg to hop along, letting a small yelp escape every few steps. When they reached the exit, they stared at the rock wall they would need to climb. Diego collapsed on the ground.

"You go," he said, defeated.

"Oh, stop," said Olivia. "We can do it."

She reached down to help Diego up as a large rock crashed in front of them, causing Olivia to trip backwards. The ground continued to violently shake as the constant rumbling grew so loudly that Olivia could barely hear her own thoughts. She had no idea how they were going to escape in one piece.

Newen appeared at the top of the crater. He sprinted toward them, skidding to a stop at the bottom. Olivia helped Diego onto the puma's back before jumping on herself. Without looking back, they began their ascent out of the crater, with Newen skillfully dodging the falling rocks around them.

After a few minutes, they reached the top, reuniting with Ruda, anxiously waiting for them, and Boldo, his normal angry expression replaced with a worried look.

"Kutral?" he asked.

"We tried," said Olivia. "He wouldn't come with us."

Newen's body sagged.

"We must go back for him!" shouted Boldo, as a large boulder shot over their heads, crashing into the glowing energy field, which began blinking off piece by piece until nothing was left.

"There's no time," said Newen. "He's on his own." He leapt forward, racing downward at full speed.

Olivia craned her neck, her eyes wide, as a huge pillar of ash rose straight up in a vertical column before expanding outward, painting the blue sky gray.

20.

ASHES, ASHES

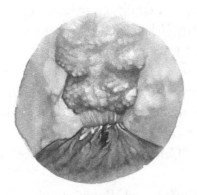

OLIVIA COULDN'T HELP but think of the first time she saw photos of the ash-covered bodies from Pompeii. She had been so mesmerized by the grisly sight that she had marched straight to the library to check out two more books on the subject. This is how she learned that the energy generated by the eruption of Mt. Vesuvius was 100,000 times stronger than an atomic bomb. Most people managed to escape this first phase of the eruption. Those who didn't, however, would meet their fate at the hands of a lightning-fast landslide of hot gas and rock known as a pyroclastic flow.

Now, fleeing a real-life volcanic eruption, Olivia wished she hadn't read so much about them. She wished that she didn't know anything about stratovolcanoes, or Pompeii, or pyroclastic flows. But she did and knew that if a pyroclastic flow *did* happen, there would be no outrunning it.

Olivia squeezed Diego tighter as a large chunk of volcanic rock crashed into the ground to their right. Newen sped on without flinching. Olivia watched as Ruda and Boldo skirted around smaller rocks that began to rain down on all sides. There was no outrunning it, as the sky began pouring pumice rain. Olivia prayed that this would be the worst of it and that the giant ash plume would continue its skyward ascent. Up and away from them.

Arriving at the clearing once more, they came to a stop. Here, at the Heart of the Forest, stood an army of animals, many more than had been present at the meeting of the River Council. There was Tucu, Maqui, the pudu family, more foxes, and even more pumas.

"The canelo berry," Maqui said with an urgent tone. "Where is it?"

Olivia reached into her pocket and felt around for the soft, round berry. As soon as she pulled it out, her heart dropped. It blinked a faint, dying glow once every five seconds.

"It can't be saved," said Boldo. He didn't look angry anymore, but terrified. "It's too late."

Ruda scoffed. "Can you be quiet for once? This is your fault after all."

"I'm sorry. I didn't know!" Boldo shrank in shame.

Ruda exhaled loudly, then did something that Olivia never would have expected. She nudged her head under Boldo's chin, as if trying to cheer him up.

"We must have faith," said Maqui in a worried tone.

Maqui hopped over to Olivia, who handed her the berry. Placing it in her cheek, she scampered along everyone's backs until she reached the Heart at the center of the clearing. As soon as Maqui jumped onto the pillar of roots, they began to untwist themselves, creating an opening in the middle, like a large woven bowl. As soon as Maqui dropped the canelo berry inside, the column of roots twisted themselves closed once more.

As everyone waited to see what would happen, a thin veil of ash swept in. Olivia coughed into her jacket sleeve, trying to soothe the burning in her throat, but it came out dry and scratchy.

A dim light blinked on from within the column of roots, but, after a split second, it went dark. After ten more seconds, it blinked once more, even fainter this time. They all waited patiently for the third blink, but it never came.

Olivia could sense the crowd of animals sag with disappointment.

"It didn't work! We must run away!" said Tique the otter. Ever the deserter, he turned and scampered off. A handful of animals followed.

"Wait! Don't go!" As Olivia stared at the horrible yet mesmerizing spectacle overhead, she understood why the animals fled. The sun was beginning to set behind the volcano, its rays of light painting the ash cloud brilliant shades of orange and red. She looked desperately toward Newen and Ruda. A layer of gray dust was beginning to coat their fur. She turned to the others, standing firmly side by side, looking at her desperately, every one of them soon to be painted gray with hot ash.

"There has to be something we can do. Anything."

"There is one thing we can try." Newen stepped forward. "It will take all of us focusing our energy on the purest of all emotions."

"Great! So which—" Olivia stopped herself. "It's love, isn't it?"

If she had heard herself say that a few days ago she would have laughed and called herself a sappy little princess. But she knew now that this was the right answer.

"These last few days, I've felt so many emotions," Olivia began. Her eyes were burning. She placed her hands in front of her face and coughed into them. "Some of them have been overwhelming, some of them terrible, but the strongest of them all has been *love*. Love for my dad, who I thought was lost, but now I know he's with me always. Love for my mom, who I thought I hated, but is the one person I've needed the most this whole time. And love for each of you. Maqui, Tucu, Ruda, Newen. And you, Diego. I thought I wouldn't make any new friends here. But somehow, despite all odds, you wormed your way into my heart!"

Still lying on Newen's back, Diego grabbed at Olivia's bomber jacket, pulling her closer. He wrapped an arm around her, and Olivia squeezed him back. Ruda joined them. Then, one by one, each of the animals moved in closer. Each one of them placed their head against the one in front. As they embraced each other, the faint trails of light traveling through them began to merge together, glowing brighter.

From the corner of her eye, Olivia could see that the column of roots was beginning to blink a little bit brighter. She squeezed her companions harder and whispered, "Please. Save them somehow."

Rocks were now raining down in hail sized pieces, clanging loudly as they hit the ground. Olivia felt dizzy and sick and unsure how much longer she could stand. Somewhere in the back of her head, an old nursery rhyme began to swell, one that never made any sense until now.

Ring around the rosie,
Pockets full of posie,
Ashes, ashes,
We all fall . . .

A bright light shot out from the pillar of roots in all directions. It shined increasingly brighter until everything was bathed in white.

A cold wet sensation on her forehead woke Olivia from a daze. She found herself on her back, looking straight up. Floating down from the sky was not the gray volcanic ash from before, but instead a flurry of pure white snow.

Olivia sat, dusting off the cold powder from her forehead. Beside her sat Diego and all the animals. One by one, they each stood and shook off the snow from their fur and feathers.

"*Mira!*" shouted Diego, pointing into the distance. A series of round lights shined in their direction. "*Nos encontraron!*"

"I don't understand."

"*Hoooooo-woo!*" Olivia's family call echoed throughout the forest.

Olivia froze. The realization hit her hard and fast. Diego was speaking Spanish. And those round lights in the distance must be from flashlights. *Humans* carrying flashlights.

That could only mean one thing. They were back, on *their* side of the forest, where there was no magical Energy allowing them to understand each other. Maybe the berry was too broken to work all the way, or maybe the forest only had enough Energy left to stop the volcano. Either way, Olivia couldn't help but feel disappointed.

The round lights grew larger. Closer.

"¡Aquí!" screamed Diego. *"¡Estamos aquí!"*

"Wait, stop," said Olivia.

She nodded toward the animals, a majority of whom had already darted into the forest. Even Maqui scampered into a nearby tree, and Tucu flew off. The only ones who remained were their closest companions, Newen and Ruda. But they had their eyes wide and ears back in fear of the approaching threat.

"¿Qué vamos a—" Diego stopped himself. "What we do?"

Olivia stood and approached Newen slowly. She knew in her gut that he wouldn't understand her, but after everything they had been through, she had to try.

"You have to go," she urged. "Quick, before they get here."

There was no response, not even a shift in Newen's steady gaze.

Ruda hopped forward. She tilted her head sideways, sniffing the air. The hair on the back of her neck stood on end.

Unable to stand, Diego grabbed the fox and pulled her in for a hug. She looked surprised at first, but soon melted into the boy's embrace. He whispered something to her in Spanish. Olivia didn't understand it, and she realized that Ruda wouldn't either. Maybe that wasn't the point.

Olivia turned back to Newen. She bent on one knee, coming eye-to-eye with the large cat. Without the ability to communicate, he now, somehow, seemed *wilder*. She couldn't help but feel a twinge of fear as she reached her hand toward him. Then, without hesitation, he stepped forward, nudging his cheek against Olivia's own.

"Thank you," she whispered, digging her fingers into the thick fur of his neck.

"Olivia! Diego!" a voice echoed through the clearing, followed by a loud bark. They were far too close.

"You have to go now," begged Olivia, standing once more. "Newen, Ruda, please."

But they refused to budge. They stood like soldiers at the ready, backs lowered, ears flat, staring in the direction of the approaching flashlights.

Max emerged from the trees. Sprinting straight toward Newen and Ruda, he barked at them. It wasn't an aggressive bark, but the one he used to greet Miss Jane's dog across the street. He then rubbed his head against Olivia's leg, like he was trying to tell them *you go. I'll protect her.*

Newen cocked his head and twitched his whiskers. He then raised his body, turned, and leapt into the forest, with Ruda following closely.

Olivia exhaled, relieved, and wrapped her arms around her dog, happy to be reunited once more. She had no idea if Max had actually *said* something to them. Either way, she was thankful that they had understood the message, somehow.

She turned to Diego, another concern popping into her head. "Our story. They're never going to believe us when we tell them what actually happened. And even if they did, we can't tell them the truth because that would put the animals at risk. We have to—"

"*Espera, espera, espera!*" said Diego "Slow down." He motioned downwards with his hands.

"Sorry. So—" Olivia exhaled, calming herself. "So they will ask us what happened. We have to lie. Understand?"

Diego nodded.

"Good. Here's what we say."

21.
New Beginning

ONE MONTH LATER

"One little word." Olivia sat nose-to-nose with Max, her hands on his cheeks. "It'll be our secret, I promise."

Squashing his cheeks together, she moved his lips up and down with her fingers. *"Heh-lo, Oh-lee-vee-ya."*

His tail swept the floor clean behind him, enjoying the extra close personal attention he was receiving. Olivia had tried every day for the past month to get Max to say something. It hadn't worked yet, but she kept at it, just in case. "Come on, Maxy, say something. Anything. Speak!"

"WOOF!" Max barked into Olivia's face before giving her one enormous lick on the cheek.

Abu cackled out a laugh from the kitchen and tossed Max a piece of sausage, which he swallowed whole. She had been extra nice to him lately, calling him *"el perro heroe"* and knitting him a large assortment of doggy clothes and even a fluffy nest-like bed, which she proudly placed in front of the fire for him.

"Te están esperando!" Abu called out, pointing her lips at the door in that funny way Chileans did. *"Pásalo bien, princesa."*

Olivia rose and gave Abu a quick kiss on the cheek. She no longer minded being called a princess, at least not when her grandmother said it. She grabbed her jacket, backpack, and new green and blue scarf Abu had knitted her, which came with a matching sweater for Max, and she and Max flew out the door. At the end of the driveway, Ma and Tata were waiting for them.

"Nice jacket." Tata winked.

Olivia grinned. She had recently asked Ma to take her shopping for a new jacket, deciding to give her father's a much-needed retirement. This new one was still green and outdoorsy, of course, but it was more her size and not covered in holes. And even though it hadn't belonged to Dad, she could still feel him with her.

They walked down the road toward Diego's house, where they found him already waiting for them outside. He sat in a wheelchair, his injured leg still healing in a cast. Beside him, his older brother stood with his hands in his front pocket. When he pulled them out to wave hello, Olivia couldn't help feeling relieved that no pet snakes emerged.

"Por fin! We wait *sooooo* long!" said Diego, teasing her.

"Oh, perdón!" retorted Olivia playfully. "Just making sure I had *todo listo."*

Despite his leg injury, Diego was still the same happy-go-lucky boy she had first met. Even though he had to forget about playing soccer for the foreseeable future, he had never seemed to mind. The cast made him the coolest kid in school, with everyone lining up to sign their name on it.

Another good thing to come out of it was that his brother was finally being nice to him. Apparently, he had been so distraught when Diego went missing, that he had given him a big apology and swore never to act like such a jerk again. Now, he double checked that Diego had everything he needed, and then bent over to give him a big hug.

"Y no te escapes esta vez!" he said, tussling Diego's hair.

"Será un poco más difícil ahora," Diego grinned, motioning to his leg.

Diego's brother said goodbye to them, then turned to walk back into the house.

"Can I drive?" Olivia grinned, grabbing the back of the wheelchair, and pulling Diego into a wheelie, making him laugh.

Tata snatched the handles from Olivia's grip. *"Mejor manejo yo,"* he chuckled.

He pushed off, and so began the familiar walk into the forest. The path was better taken care of now, wider even. After about twenty minutes, they arrived at a large wooden sign that read *PARQUE ALERCE ANDINO.* Below was a map of the park as well as a description of all of the flora and fauna it contained. Fauna which, not so long ago, had not been there at all.

"I can't believe it really happened," said Olivia.

"You did it, honey," said Ma, flashing her big, beautiful smile.

"We all did," said Olivia, smiling back.

After they had returned from their adventure in the forest, the newspapers and local television channels had all wanted to interview the two missing children about what happened. Every time, they both said the same thing, that they survived thanks to the animals. Animals who saved them from the storm, fed them, sheltered them, and took them in as their own.

They left out the crazy parts, of course. Even then, there were some people who still didn't believe them. But most people fell completely in love with their incredible story. So much so that when Olivia and Diego started an online petition to protect the forest, it quickly racked up over half a million signatures. The public's support became so strong that within weeks the government had classified the forest as a protected land and began the paperwork to declare it a national park.

After a ten-minute walk down the trail, they arrived at the campsite. There were already four other families present, all of them from Olivia and Diego's school. Their classmates greeted them excitedly as the adults set up their tents. Once done, Tata called them over and asked if they each remembered to bring their bag of seeds.

Carolina, Germán, Raúl and Cris had brought an assortment of seeds from different native trees—alerce, arrayán, coigüe, and avellano. When it was Olivia and Diego's turn to reveal which seeds they had chosen, they both held their bags high in the air and yelled, "Canelo!"

The children then split in twos, each pair headed off in a different direction, accompanied by at least one adult. Olivia and Diego, now on crutches, headed north with Tata and Ma. Eventually, they reached the location where Olivia had found Tata yelling at the loggers. The ground was bare except for dozens of tree stumps and crumpled ferns. Tata sighed.

"Does it make you sad, Tata?" Olivia asked.

"No." He looked at her and smiled. "First time in many years, I feel . . . *esperanza.*" He beat his chest with his fist gently.

They each dug their fingers into a bag and pulled out a handful of seeds, which they sprinkled on the ground. Max pranced around them, trying to catch a few in his mouth as if it were kibble. Olivia watched him, giggling. An idea struck her.

"Max, come!" she called. He trotted over and plopped himself in front of her, tongue out.

Olivia bent down and fiddled with his collar until she managed to unhook the metal ring around his nametag. She pierced one end through her plastic seed bag and rehooked it to his collar, letting the bag dangle from his neck. Olivia then ripped a small hole in the bottom of the bag and watched a few seeds pour out.

Grabbing a stick from the ground, she tossed it as far as she could. Max sprinted after it, seeds spilling out as he ran.

Tata boomed out a laugh and yelled, *"Maravilloso!"*

They continued dispersing seeds for almost an hour, until Diego got tired of leaning on his crutches and Max got tired of chasing sticks.

"One more," Olivia said, holding the stick out to Tata. "Throw it super far!"

Tata chucked the stick as far as he could, and Max sprinted out of view. After a minute, he called out three long barks. Without thinking, Olivia raced after him, ignoring Tata and Ma's shouts of "NO!"

Pummeling through ferns and bushes, all Olivia could think was, *not again. I'm not losing him again.* Arriving at another clearing, she came to a halt.

There he was, staring into the trees in front of him. Olivia frowned.

"Max, what is it?"

"Woof!" he barked, tail wagging.

Olivia held her breath as she stepped forward. *Could it be? Could it really be . . . them?* She took another step cautiously, squinting into the dark tangle of greens. She tried not to get her hopes up. Max barked at nothing all the time. *It was probably . . .*

There! She saw them, two emerald eyes twinkling in the dark, staring right at her. To their right and lower to the ground, two gold eyes blinked at her. She knew those eyes. They were unmistakable. A few more steps, and she would see them, touch them even . . .

A rustling of leaves behind her made Olivia jump.

Tata emerged from the trees, out of breath. He collapsed to his knees and grabbed Olivia's arms tightly.

"Nunca mas hagas eso!" He threw his arms around her and breathed deeply.

"Oh! I'm sorry! I didn't mean to—" Olivia twisted her head around, but the eyes were already gone. She sighed.

She knew that, like any other wild animal, it was best that they stay hidden and safe from harm. But she couldn't deny how badly she had yearned to see them again, nor how fast her heart had beaten from those few short-lived seconds of excitement. Although much too brief for her liking, it would have to be enough. For now.

After Tata and Olivia rejoined Ma and Diego, and Olivia repeated her promise to never ever run off like that again, they all began their trek back to camp. Too tired to walk, Diego piggybacked on Tata's back. After a minute, he kicked Olivia in the side, raising his eyebrows with an unspoken question. Olivia nodded, and Diego smiled wider than she'd ever seen.

By the time they got back to camp, the orange sun was already low in the sky. Tata sat Diego back in his wheelchair and began gathering a bundle of dry sticks. He threw them in the middle of the clearing and asked the children who wanted to learn to build a *fogata*. The other children jumped up and raised their hands as Diego and Olivia shared a knowing look.

As the fire grew stronger, Ma unpacked an old metal tea kettle. She filled it with two cartons of milk and set it on a rock close to the flames. She then unpacked a half-dozen small metal mugs and, saving the best for last, a big box of chocolate bars.

"Quién quiere un submarino de chocolate?" She grinned.

As the other children ran to receive their mugs and portions of chocolate, Olivia studied Ma's smile. She had never noticed that it was a little bit crooked, like something was weighing it down on one side. Such a tiny imperfection made her think that maybe even Peppy Pepa couldn't be perfectly happy all the time. Maybe she was only trying her best, like everyone else. And maybe that was enough.

As everyone sat around sipping their chocolate submarines and telling ghost stories, Olivia thought of how much her father would have loved being here. She reached her hand into her pocket and pulled out a marble. It was the same one that Diego had broken with his slingshot on the day they first met. Olivia had glued the two pieces back together and saved it for this moment. She rolled it between her fingers, seeing how the light from the campfire flickered off its glass surface. The crack was still visible, but that only made it more interesting, like it had a story to tell.

Olivia dug her fingers into the cold earth and pushed a hole into the center. She then dropped the marble in the middle and gently covered it with dirt. It wasn't a seed, but it was still a new beginning. As she patted the soil, she thought she saw a flicker of light run up her arm. She squinted, waiting for another, but none came.

Must have been from the fire, Olivia thought. She reached for another chocolate bar, trying to ignore her disappointment.

"Mmmm chocolate," whispered a voice that Olivia could have sworn sounded like . . .

Max stared directly at the chocolate in her hand, a long strand of drool spilling out of his mouth.

Olivia waved it in front of him. "Is this what you want, Maxy?"

He looked at her with large, pleading eyes, but no words came.

"Livy, you know he can't, honey," said Ma.

"I know, I was only checking if . . . nevermind." Olivia smiled, biting off a chunk of chocolate. Immediately the familiar warmth formed in her stomach. But along with this warmth, there was another feeling, something Tata had said—*esperanza*. Hope.

Lying in her mother's lap, she stared up at the moon. As Ma's skinny fingers combed themselves through her hair, Olivia swore that somewhere between the glittering stars and the dark tangle of branches, two bright yellow eyes were staring down at her.

Afterword

MANY ELEMENTS FROM this book were inspired by the Mapuche indigenous people, whose beautiful animal-filled fables (*epew*) teach important values such as strength, love, wisdom, and community.

The animals Newen (puma), Ruda (fox), and Tucu (owl) were inspired by real animals living in Fundación Romahue, an animal rescue center in Puerto Varas, Chile (Northern Patagonia). Newen, which means *strength* in the Mapuche language *Mapudungun*, lives with two other rescued pumas, Lolo and Ayún, all of whom lost their mothers when they were cubs. Ruda the grey fox really does have a missing paw but hasn't let that stop her from becoming the leader of the other foxes. Tucu the owl can always be found atop his favorite perch upon the tallest branch. His large yellow eyes constantly follow visitors throughout the center.

The ongoing loss of these animals' habitats continues to be a severe problem throughout Patagonia. Carnivores such as wild cats and foxes are especially harmed as humans continue to expand into their territory.

Along with traditional conservation methods such as designating protected lands, continuing the Mapuche tradition of telling stories involving positive human-animal relationships could also prove to be a creative way to teach the younger generations about wildlife conservation.

ACKNOWLEDGMENTS

THANK YOU TO the staff of Fundación Romahue animal rescue center for introducing me to the animals who would one day inspire my story. What you do is important and has roots far beyond what you see.

Thank you to Erin Becker, Nora Boydston, Bidisha Chakraborty, and Sandra Steiger; without you amazing weirdos of my writing Coven, where would I be? Thank you to my *madrina* Wendolín Perla for always believing in me more enthusiastically than I believed in myself. If I ever needed an emotional boost, I knew who to go to.

Thank you to the photographers who allowed me to use their wildlife photos as reference for my illustrations—Vicente Valdés (otter) and Eduardo Minte (kodkod) and Gustavo Latorre (puma, fox, owl).

Thank you to my early beta readers—Aimee, Magdalena, Bidisha, Moises, Anita, Tova, and Drake. Special thanks to my amazing niblings Lillian and Elijah Willis, and my sister Kimmi Pierce, for allowing me to read my book to you out loud, which was one of my favorite experiences of all time. Your feedback was invaluable, and your love of my story pushed me forward.

All my love to my family who bestowed me with a love of art, animals, and fantasy worlds. Thank you to my grandmother, Laura Weaver Huff, and mother, Patty Koehler, for taking me to go draw animals at the zoo, where the big cats were always my favorite. Thank

you to my father, John Koehler, for wielding a relentless red pen on my writing from a young age. To you and Joe Coccaro, thank you for believing in me enough to put my book out into the world.

Thank you to my Chilean adoptive family for sharing your love of this beautiful country and culture with me and making this *gringuita* feel at home here.

And of course, my eternal love and gratitude to my husband, Gustavo, for not only supporting me throughout two-plus years of obsessive writing, rewriting, editing, drawing, painting (rinse and repeat), but for always fueling my curiosity and creativity, for pushing me to sign up for art classes, for taking wildlife photos for me to draw, and for always saying yes to the next adventure together.

CPSIA information can be obtained
at www.ICGtesting.com
Printed in the USA
LVHW111705100921
697555LV00019B/564/J